BILLIONAIRE'S CAPTIVE MISTRESS

Kings of the Underworld Book 1

NIKITA SLATER

AUTHOR'S NOTE

Dear readers,

Billionaire's Captive Mistress was originally published in 2016 as King's Command, Fire & Vice book 3. I gave the entire series an update including new covers, new titles, new series title, and an updated proofread. The material remains the same.

This series is dark romance with strong alpha anti-heroes with jealous possessive tendencies. The women are strong and feisty, not easily wooed by these bad men (hence the captive romance part!).

Thank you for choosing Billionaire's Captive Mistress. I hope you enjoy!

XOXO,

Nikita

CHAPTER ONE

Tyson King felt her presence the moment she stepped across the threshold and into the city's most dangerous illegal gambling den. His shoulders stiffened as he glanced up and spotted her. Tyson didn't so much as twitch a muscle to give away his sudden tension, but his bodyguard, Daniel Mercer, went instantly to attention and scanned the room. Tyson knew the moment his deadly man set eyes on Claudia Cantore, because his alarm dropped and he relaxed back into position behind Tyson.

Tyson forcibly quelled the surge of jealous rage that flared to life as male eyes all over the room focused on her. The tall, beautiful blond was starting to draw stares from some of the city's most dangerous men. Tonight Claudia had packed her delicious curves into a thigh length blue bandage dress with her waist length honey-coloured hair flowing loose around her bare shoulders. Her long legs were made longer by the four-inch spiked, black heels she wore.

His rational self acknowledged that she was a stunning woman who drew stares no matter where she went. Still, he found himself wanting to stalk across the room toward her, drag her home and spank her ass for daring to wear that dress in public, let alone in a room full of hardened males with power-privilege complexes. The only thing stopping him was that she had no idea who he was or why he felt the intense need to keep her locked away for himself.

He watched her, his dark eyes following every movement of her graceful body, every breath she took in that tiny dress. His calculating brain went over his acquisition plan once more, assuring himself he would eventually possess the woman who had consumed his thoughts these past three months. He hadn't become a billionaire from rash behaviour, but from calmly, ruthlessly acquiring things that made him rich. Now he applied that strategy to something that he wanted: Claudia Cantore.

Her eyes met his. He didn't break his stare, enjoying the tiny flare to her eyes before she nervously broke contact and turned to her friend, Anastasia Sitnikov, to speak in low tones. When Anastasia turned to look where her friend was gesturing, he saw the recognition and instant alarm on her petite features. Interesting. The mob princess knew exactly who he was and of his ruthless reputation.

Unfortunately, he suspected she was in the process of telling Claudia to keep her distance from him, which would make his plans to woo the blond beauty slightly more difficult. He had enough information on his quarry to potentially blackmail her into his bed, but he had planned on using more subtle measures. There was a softness to her – of looks and personality – and he didn't want to spoil it. He wanted her willing.

Tyson rapidly calculated the odds of Claudia coming to him easily with Anastasia's condemnation now contaminating any future contact between them. Claudia was a suspicious woman, if somewhat naïve. Her colourful past leant her an edge, despite her softness. She didn't make friends easily, and the fact that she willingly followed the Sitnikov girl into a seedy gambling den told him that she would listen to her friend when she told her to stay away from Tyson King.

With an annoyed sigh, Tyson picked up his water glass and swallowed half of the liquid before placing the glass carefully on the table. He wanted a cigar, but smoking wasn't allowed in the club, an amusing fact considering the illegal nature of the underground casino's existence. Khalid Mahdavi, the current owner, didn't enjoy the smell stinking up his establishments. Tyson's finger twitched around the unopened Cohiba he had placed on the table in anticipation of a smoke break before his next round.

The smoke would have to wait. He wasn't willing to leave Claudia in the room unprotected with some of the most unscrupulous men the city could scrape up. His eyes tracked the woman as she followed her smaller friend across the floor toward a table with two empty spots. He frowned fiercely, disliking the way she so easily turned her back on him, dismissing him from her thoughts once Anastasia had warned her away. As the women approached, the men at the table all but drooled on themselves in their hurry to have two attractive ladies buy into their game. Tyson wanted to murder them all.

Movement at the small bar set in the corner of the club caught his attention, tearing his eyes from Claudia. Another man watched her with an intensity that instantly had Tyson's blood pressure rising. But this guy wasn't watching her the way the others were. His greedy eyes were cold with material lust over sexual interest. His eyes devoured her every move, like she was his payday. *Shit*. Tyson had hoped he'd have more time.

He leaned back, big body causing the chair underneath him to creak in protest, and turned his head to Mercer who leaned in to listen. "My plans involving the woman have changed. See the Hispanic man at the bar?" Mercer nodded, his deadly gaze riveting to the guy whose eyes were on King's woman. The guy took out a cell phone and dialled as the two men watched. "Get Mike to bring the car around. She may not exit willingly. Be ready, I want this smooth and quiet."

Mercer nodded in understanding and straightened, pulling his phone out to text the driver. The ex-guerrilla knew how to read situations with brutal clarity. Knowing Tyson's interest in Claudia Cantore, he probably assumed the plans had changed the moment she stepped foot in the club, a place she clearly didn't belong, where trouble could so easily find her. If Mercer were known for softer emotions, let alone any kind of emotion, he might feel pity for the woman who had unknowingly captured the attention of the city's kingpin.

The two women had joined a lower stakes poker game and played for several minutes when Tyson noticed an irate Asher Bowles stalking toward the game, his eyes locked on the women. Tyson tensed, as did Mercer at his back. Mercer may have become friendly with the lethal fighter, but he knew his boss wasn't going to allow interference with the woman, which was part of the reason Tyson utterly trusted the deadly bodyguard. Mercer's last loyalty always lay with Tyson King.

Ash approached the table and stood directly behind Anastasia Sitnikov's chair, staring down at her with a mixture of fury and intense longing. This was an interesting development that Tyson would have to look into further. So far as he had known, Ash and the Sitnikov girl had no common interests. She tended to lay low for the most part, well hidden under her brother's protective wing. Unless the Russian's were looking for a new fighter to add to their roster; Ash was the best the state had to offer.

Tyson watched dispassionately as Anastasia turned in her chair to confront the big man that looked like he both wanted to tear her apart and eat her up. She looked coldly dismissive of whatever Ash was saying to her, which visibly infuriated the usually unflappable man. Interesting.

Claudia had been watching the exchange between the two with hesitant interest, her green eyes wide with frightened uncertainty. Anastasia took her hand and stood with Claudia to face Ash. They were two small morsels facing off with the lethal championship fighter.

Tyson stood and jerked his head toward the exit. "Meet me at the car."

Mercer nodded and, without another glance around, followed Tyson's orders, both spoken and unspoken. He would make sure his boss and the woman could make a swift and quiet exit.

Tyson kept his eyes glued to the situation unfolding across the room as he stalked around tables to reach Claudia. Though he had no idea what was happening between Ash and the Russian girl, he wasn't impressed that his woman was being dragged into things. It would likely save Ash's life that he, and the rest of the city besides Mercer, had no clue that Tyson King was staking a claim on Claudia Cantore. Once the news became known, anyone that dared speak to her without his permission would face swift and brutal consequences.

Claudia watched the conversation between her friend and the huge fighter with breathless anxiety. It was clear she had no idea what she could do to help Anastasia, but the woman attempted to back her friend both physically and verbally by snapping at Ash while clinging to her friend. Tyson hurried toward them, worried that Ash would strike out at the lovely blond trying to protect her friend. To his relief, Ash only looked darkly amused by her outburst.

Tyson arrived in time to prevent her from taking her

tirade against Ash further. Sensing his presence behind her, Claudia tensed from head to toe and spun around to face him. Her wide eyes collided with his chest only inches from her face. She stared at him in shock and trepidation.

Satisfaction flooded him as she laid eyes on him up close for the first time. Her nervous gaze took in his massive proportions and widened in fear and curiosity.

"Is there a problem here?" his deep voice rumbled over her head.

Claudia stumbled back against Anastasia and watched as he challenged Ash. Tyson could only imagine what she thought of him. He was a big, dark-skinned, scarred up man who took what he wanted using any method that would work in his favour. As a result, violence surrounded him like a cloak, usually terrifying those that didn't know him. Once they knew him better, and their opinions of his brutality were confirmed, they tended to think even more harshly of him. Usually that worked for him, but it was unfortunate that he might now frighten Claudia.

Ash didn't back down. Instead, he nodded. "I need to have a conversation with my woman here, in private."

King took in the situation at a glance. Ash had clearly staked his claim on Anastasia Sitnikov, which was perhaps a very stupid thing to do, given her mob connections, but Tyson had to admire his guts. He nodded, "I can take care of the other one."

"No!" Claudia gasped.

Tyson swallowed his instant annoyance at her denial. He reminded himself that he would need to show a little patience with her. She didn't know who he was or what he was capable of. Soon enough she would learn not to deny him anything, if she wanted to live a happy, comfortable life.

"Thanks man, I owe you," Ash said, reaching for Anastasia and jerking her into his arms. He began dragging her away from the table toward the club exit.

"Hey!" Claudia cried out, starting to go after her friend. Tyson placed a heavy hand on her shoulder and pinned her in place. A shudder rippled through her body at the contact. His grip tightened and he had to remind himself to go gently now that he finally had Claudia Cantore in his grasp. He turned her around to face him.

Studying her face, he wrapped long, thick fingers around her slender throat and tilted her chin up with a caressing thumb. He watched the angry, frightened green eyes flare in challenge. He'd never wanted a woman more than he wanted this one. And he finally had the leverage he needed. It was perhaps a stroke of luck that the woman he'd been investigating since seeing her at one of the banks he owned several weeks ago happened to wander into the club he was about to purchase.

"Come," he said to her, releasing her neck and taking a firm grip on her arm. "Let's talk."

Claudia gasped and went with him. He gave her no choice. She tried resisting his hold, but it was unbreakable. "We have nothing to discuss Mr. King," she hissed. "Let go of my arm!"

Tyson gave her a predatory smile and said, "We have everything to discuss Miss Cantore. Starting with your protection fee. If I was able to find out who you are, it's a certainty that other interested parties could also find out."

As they walked Tyson indicated the man at the bar whose gaze never once wavered from his prey, the beauty in the blue dress. Tyson stared at the man with such cold malevolence the guy immediately turned away from them, hunching his shoulders and leaning against the bar. He spoke into his phone in rapid Spanish.

Claudia stared up at Tyson, understanding changing her

expression from anger to absolute terror. She went with him unresistingly, but her tense body was still ready for flight. He held her tightly, enjoying the softness of her skin beneath his fingers. Fierce hunger burned within him as he touched her for the first time, admitting that the change in his original plan was a good thing. It was time to stop gathering information on Claudia and take the woman herself.

"Get in the car, Claudia," he said calmly, as though he weren't essentially kidnapping her.

A sudden thought sent spears of terror through her body. What if he was taking her to Dante, or worse, Franco Delgado? Both men had reason to want her dead. She had no idea what Tyson King's connections might be, but she suspected his reach was far. The way he spoke of 'protection' made her think he knew at least part of her past.

"Please," she said, looking up into his dark, forbidding face. "Just leave me here, I can find my own way home. I promise, I'll go straight there and not return to this club ever again." She would go straight home, grab some essentials and then get the first flight out of here.

Tyson's gravelly laugh dashed her hopes of an easy escape. "You need to get in the car, beautiful. I'm not letting you go."

His words sounded so final. He put more pressure on her arm, pushing her toward the open door of the car. In a desperate attempt to break his hold, Claudia threw her elbow back into his hard stomach and then wrenched her body sideways, away from the open door. Tyson's breath whooshed out at the impact, but his grip didn't slacken in the least, nor did he move an inch when she threw herself away from him. All Claudia managed to accomplish was to knock herself off balance. If he hadn't been holding her so tightly she would have hit the pavement hard. Instead, only her hand and the tips of her long blond hair grazed the ground.

With a grunt of annoyance, Tyson hauled her upright, then bodily picked her up as though she weighed no more than a child. Before Claudia could even think to struggle, the other man placed a hand on her head to protect her from the doorframe while Tyson shoved her through the door and climbed in the car behind her.

As the doors slammed shut, Claudia let out a scream of fear, which was immediately cut off by Tyson's giant hand

CHAPTER TWO

"I don't know what you're talking about." Claudia tried to make her voice sound normal as she was steered toward the front entrance of the gambling club she had foolishly allowed herself to be dragged to.

Cool air washed over her heated skin when they stepped out of the club and into the dark night. She shivered and blinked several times, trying to adjust her eyes to the sudden darkness. The man that held her arm in a vice grip, Tyson King, ignored her words completely. He looked around impatiently, his sharp eyes taking in the traffic on the street, and then dragged her toward a car parked at the curb.

Another man, not as big as Tyson but just as frightening, opened the door to the car. This guy had a brutal, chilling look about him that made Claudia shiver. He looked like he ate babies for breakfast, women for lunch and Navy Seals for supper. There was no way she was getting in the car with these people. Claudia tried to pull away from Tyson, digging her heels against the pavement. Tyson stopped abruptly and looked down at her.

against her mouth. She began to struggle, reaching for the latch on the other door closest to her. He held her tightly against his huge body as the car pulled away from the curb and sped from the club.

Claudia's struggles began to calm. Tyson's hold was unbreakable and all she was managing to do was wiggle her body all over his chest and lap. Her chest heaved with fear and exertion. His scent, mint combined with a hint of cigar, enveloped her. Lightheadedness blurred her vision from his heavy hand cutting off most of her air supply and her body gradually relaxed into limpness.

"Will you scream if I move my hand?" his husky voice whispered in her ear.

Claudia squeezed her eyes shut, trying to keep the tears that sprang to her eyes at bay. She shook her head slightly in his tight hold. He eased the pressure as though to test her and then removed his hand completely when she didn't scream. Her back was to his chest and his thick arm was wrapped around her middle. The bottom of her dress had hiked up a few very important inches in her struggle to be free. The result was a wealth of pale skin and long legs sprawled out over his knees. With her arms trapped at her sides, she couldn't attempt to pull the skirt back down to a decent length. She tried squirming a little, hoping she might be able to loosen his hold in the roomy back seat so she could crawl off his lap.

The only noticeable effect her fidgeting had on him was the *huge* erection she felt growing against her backside. She froze, her breathing becoming shallow as a new fear sprang to her mind. He had been staring at her with such intensity in the club. Did he want her in that way? These men could do anything to her. The only people she knew in the city were Anya and her boss at the café. The small Russian woman was still a mystery to her, and her boss knew so little about her she likely wouldn't have the first clue where to look if Claudia disappeared. Not one other person in the world knew she existed here.

The three men in the car looked like hardened criminals to her eyes. She had no doubt each one of them had engaged in heinous acts prior to kidnapping her, especially the one that had touched her head. The aura of violence surrounding him was so intense that she was sure people gave him a wide berth when he was out in public. An imaginary band tightened around her chest, constricting her breathing. How did she manage to get herself into these messes?

"Breathe, Claudia," Tyson's voice rumbled in her ear again, his breath stirring the hair against her temple.

Claudia shivered, but nonetheless tried to get more air into her starved lungs. Something about his calm voice reassured her that she wasn't about to become a statistic of random violence. Even if she were in trouble, she would need a clear head to fight her way out if a chance for escape presented itself.

His movements swift and sure, Tyson shifted her off his lap and into the seat next to him. When his hands reached for the skirt of her dress, Claudia's much smaller hands flew to his wrists automatically and pulled uselessly. He only tugged the skirt down a few precious inches, surprising her. He placed the small clutch purse she had been carrying with her in her lap and then reached around her to pull a seatbelt across her upper body and engage the latch. He did the same with his own belt then turned to face her.

The whites of his eyes were the only part of his face she could make out clearly in the darkness. They were firmly fixed on her.

"The door lock is engaged on the inside, don't bother trying to open that door until it's released," he said.

Her tense body relaxed slightly. She had indeed planned

on waiting for the car to slow down enough that she might be able to somehow get her seatbelt off, the door open and then jump into the road before he could grab her again. It was an unlikely plan, but it was all she had. She found his statement almost reassuring. She hadn't been looking forward to the amount of her bare skin that might come in contact with the pavement if the car was moving when she managed to get out.

"Why are you doing this? Where are you taking me?" she asked, glancing out the window at the passing buildings. The club had been located in a somewhat unsavoury area of downtown. They were speeding past the dilapidated buildings toward the nicer end next to the river.

He ignored her first question, but answered the second. "We're going to my penthouse."

Claudia shifted in her seat, edging her knees away from where they rested close to his. He was such a big man that his body filled most of the roomy back seat of the vehicle. If she had to guess, she would say he was around 6'4" and close to 300 lbs. She wasn't a small woman, but he had held her as easily as he might a child. One of his massive fists could easily kill her with one blow.

As if sensing her discomfort, he spoke easily. "I'm not going to hurt you, Claudia. That was never my intention."

"What *is* your intention then?" she demanded, trying to make her voice sound snappy, but she knew the waver ruined any hope she had of sounding like she was in complete control of herself. "Because forcing me out of that club and into your car isn't a very good start at convincing me of your good intentions."

He only continued to stare at her and she thought he might not answer. Finally, his deep voice rumbled, "I didn't say my intentions were good, just that I have no intention of hurting you in particular. Don't make the mistake of thinking I might be a respectable man, Claudia. Keep that in mind."

Claudia shivered and glanced toward the front seat. The other two men were ignoring the pair in the back seat as though their jobs were that of statue and driver. That was exactly what they were, she realized, employees of Tyson King. They weren't his friends. This thought wasn't a comforting one. Friends might argue with Tyson's decisions regarding to the woman he had plucked out of the club and forced into his car. Loyal employees would follow his orders blindly. Which includes helping him make a woman disappear quietly.

"Stop worrying," he said, "there's nothing you can do right now. Just relax, we'll be there soon, then we can talk."

She sensed he wanted to reach out and touch her, but was holding back in an attempt to avoid frightening her further, which confused her. Upon brief acquaintance with him, she suspected he was the type of person that didn't care what others thought of him. That he took what he wanted without consideration of others, much the way he had snatched her up. But rather than doing what he wanted with her, he was holding back. For now, anyway.

They turned into the parking garage of one of the most exclusive high rises in the city. Claudia stared up in awe at the monstrous tower through her side window as they waited for the garage door to slide open before driving inside. Maybe once they were parked and out of the car she could try to alert someone to her plight, if there was anyone in the parking area. At the very least, she could make sure she was seen by one of the security cameras.

Rather than parking though, the driver steered the car toward what looked like a huge industrial elevator. Momentarily forgetting her immediate problem, Claudia's jaw dropped as the huge doors, opened and the car was driven onto a platform. The doors closed with a bang and a jerk as she felt the uneasy sensation of being transported upward in an elevator. She gasped and continued to look out of her window into the brightly lit car lift as it ascended. She had no idea this sort of thing existed except for in James Bond type movies.

After a minute the doors opened onto what could only be a private garage near the top of the high rise. Other cars filled the garage, drawing Claudia's notice. She wasn't even close to a car expert. And while she didn't know what kind of car they were in now, she thought she saw a sleek black Jaguar, a red Ferrari, what looked like an older model Mercedes and several black SUVs with dark tinted windows.

Her shocked gaze met Tyson's. Who was he? And what the heck did he want with her? He looked back at her, his eyes dark and probing, as though trying to divine her thoughts.

The driver parked the car in a spot near a set of glass double doors leading into some kind of private lobby. Tyson unbuckled her seatbelt and pulled her across his seat to leave through his door. Taking hold of her arm once more, he led them through the doors and into the lobby with another set of elevators.

His hold was less a way of making sure she wouldn't run again and more of a proprietary touch. Where could she run to anyway, she thought bitterly? She suspected she wouldn't be able to find her way out of this massive penthouse space even if she spent a few days trying, let alone the seconds she might actually have if she was able to somehow break his hold on her arm.

Tyson turned to his men, "I'm finished with you both for the night. I'll call tomorrow if I need anything. Mercer, no one disturbs us tonight."

Both men nodded, though Mercer's piercing golden eyes

met Claudia's for a split second. The coldness there nearly made her step closer to Tyson for protection against his protection. Mercer might be good-looking in the classical sense with a bearded, chiseled jaw and high cheekbones – better looking even than Tyson King – but his terrifying demeanour would certainly stop a woman's gaze from lingering. Claudia would be happy if she never set eyes on him again.

She hoped fervently that she could resolve this situation with Tyson quickly and get away from his scary empire unscathed. If she managed that, she vowed to move to the middle of nowhere and become a recluse. Maybe then she would manage to stop getting mixed up with mob types.

Tyson's men took an elevator. She noticed the light above the other elevator indicated the others were going down. They were probably on the top floor of the building. She shivered, beginning to feel like Rapunzel, trapped in a tower. Only she was trapped *with* the bad guy and she feared he would kill any prince that tried to steal her away.

"Come," he said, turning toward a door at the end of the hallway.

Claudia had no idea what to expect when they entered his home, but she had assumed from the evidence of his wealth so far that it would be ostentatious. She was surprised to find that, while it was certainly grand, it was furnished with rusticity in mind, almost like a very expensively decorated cabin. The high ceilings sported wooden beams that ran from one end of the open floor plan to the other. The stainless steel kitchen dominated one section of the room while the rest was dedicated to plush leather furniture, a massive fireplace and wood flooring. Once more forgetting that she was possibly the victim of a kidnapping, Claudia stepped into the penthouse and stared around with unconcealed appreciation.

"You like it," he said, his words a statement rather than a question.

She nodded, stepping over to the windows to stare out at the sprawling view of the city below. "It's beautiful," she murmured.

"Good," he said, coming up beside her. Only, rather than the view, he stared at her, his eyes glowing in appreciation. "It's important that you like it here."

Claudia tilted her head up to look at him, heat from his body reaching out to warm her chilled skin. Though she wanted to hate everything about him, a part of her revelled in the warmth, wanting to step closer and seek more of that heat.

"Why?" she whispered. "Why is it important that I like it here?"

He reached up to touch the softness of her cheek and run a finger down the side of her neck until it rested across the delicate skin over her collarbone. She shivered at the contact. It felt good, but the underlying possessiveness of his light touch wasn't lost on her.

"Because you'll be staying here with me, Claudia."

CHAPTER THREE

She had known on an instinctual level that the man wanted her, so she wasn't entirely surprised by his response. She stepped back, attempting to put space between them. His hand dropped from her, but his knuckles brushed across the peak of her breast, tightly wrapped in the dress. Her body responded involuntarily, a spear of attraction shooting through her.

"What if I say no?" she asked, breathlessly. "What if I want to leave? Will you let me go?" She knew the answer before he spoke.

"No, I'm afraid that's not an option, Claudia."

"Why?" she asked, the constrictive band tightening around her chest once more. "That's... that's kidnapping."

He stepped back, pulling his suit jacket off his huge shoulders and laying it casually across the back of a couch. "For several reasons," he spoke, as he pulled cufflinks off his shirt, dropped them into his pocket and rolled the white sleeves of his dress shirt up his muscular forearms. Dark tattoos swirled up his arms drawing her eyes. They looked both beautiful and pagan. "I want you here, and I always get what I want, Claudia."

Short gasps of breath escaped her. "But why do you want me here?"

He swept her entire body with a long appreciative look, his eyes taking in every curve. "You're a very beautiful woman Claudia, you're every man's fantasy come to life. I think it would be fairly obvious why I would want you here in my penthouse."

Claudia wasn't a particularly self-effacing type of woman, however she wouldn't have described herself in quite that way. She was slightly overweight, not something she had a problem with, but she wouldn't think in a world that adored super thin model-like women that she would particularly draw the notice of a man of Tyson King's caliber. Her hair was too long and un-styled to be considered fashionable and her features were even, but not particularly remarkable.

"But why like this?" she asked. "Why would you force me to come here? Why wouldn't you just ask me out like a normal guy?"

"Would you have agreed to go out with me if I had walked up to you at that coffee shop you work at and asked you out on a date? Could you see us going to dinner and a movie?" he demanded. "Tell me honestly, what would your answer have been?"

She eyed his massive proportions, took note of the intense sexuality and barely leashed violence in his demeanour and shook her head. She bit her lip and answered truthfully. "I probably would have said no."

He nodded, not disturbed by her response.

"I still don't understand why you've brought me here, tonight," she persisted.

He sighed and rubbed a huge hand over his dark hair. "I saw you several weeks ago at one of my banks and had planned on pursuing you in a somewhat normal manner. Of course, I had to do a background check on you to find out if there were any flags I should be aware of before proceeding with an intimate relationship."

She frowned at his casual invasion of her privacy, remembering that particular bank trip she had taken. She usually banked online, but she'd needed to upgrade her debit card and had gone into the King Financial branch to replace her current card. She hadn't seen Tyson King. She would definitely have noticed a man that looked like a vicious linebacker wearing an expensive business suit.

"When I received the report," he continued, "I was somewhat concerned by the lack of information in Claudia Cantore's past. It's rather convenient that her parents died in a car crash when she was eighteen, leaving her with enough money to live independently and mostly off the radar. Also interesting is the lack of information about her past residences. It's almost as though she didn't exist before she popped up here eight months ago, that her past was a convenient and incredibly normal story. Too much so."

Panic flashed across Claudia's face before the expression was smothered with a neutral look. "I don't know what you're talking about."

Ignoring her denial, he continued. "I pulled a few strings among my government contacts and found out that Claudia Cantore doesn't actually exist. That she's an alias for Alicia Pedersen, a twenty-nine year old woman who was born and raised in Victoria, British Columbia, Canada. A woman whose parents are very much alive and worried sick about their missing daughter."

Darkness started to engulf Claudia's vision and she swayed, reaching blindly for something to hold on to. Without realizing it, she grabbed hold of his arm as he reached for her. Gasping, breathy sobs escaped her lips unbidden. She brought a hand up to cover her mouth and tried to force her body upright, tried to tell herself she needed to face this man who knew too much about her with all of her strength restored. But the enticing blackness surrounding her vision called to her.

She felt the world tilt beneath her and thought she must be fainting when the buttery softness of the leather couch met her back. Tyson had lifted her up, placed her on the couch and now stood over her frowning. He left her for a moment and returned with a glass. He lifted her head and shoulders with an arm around her back and placed the glass against her lips.

"Drink," he said softly.

Claudia did as he told her and sipped the liquid. As she suspected, it was whisky, which burned a path from her throat down to her belly. Warmth spread across her clammy skin, chasing away the chill of his words. She leaned up, away from the muscular bulge of his arm. She grimaced at the taste of the strong liquor. But desirous of the courage it would give her, she wrapped her fingers around the glass, taking it from Tyson. When he stepped away from the couch, she curled her legs under her and huddled into the corner.

Sipping at the whisky, she looked up at him. He stood towering over her, frowning fiercely. His arms, crossed in front of him, emphasized the bulk of muscles that rippled up his arms and chest. Ordinarily she could appreciate the view, but at the moment she was far too worried about her immediate future.

"What... what else did you find out about me?" she asked, frightened of finding out, but knowing she didn't have a choice. She had to understand what kind of a threat Tyson King constituted in her world, besides the fact that he wanted to have sex with her.

He studied her face, still frowning. "I'm not sure we

should continue this now. You came damn close to fainting when I said your real name and mentioned your parents. I'm not sure if you're up to hearing more."

"Please," she begged softly, "I have to know what I'm up against. I need to know exactly how much danger I'm in."

His frown turned even darker and he dropped to one knee in front of her. He was so tall that, even kneeling, his head still topped hers by several inches. He placed an arm across the cushion next to her body and the other one gripped the back of the couch on the other side of her head, trapping her.

"You need to understand one thing here, Claudia. You're in the safest place you can possibly be at the moment. No one can harm a hair on your head as long as you're under my protection."

"Am I?" she asked breathlessly. "Under your protection, I mean?"

"Baby, you had my protection the moment I looked up and saw you standing in line at the bank, smiling and chatting with the complete stranger behind you," his deep voice rumbled.

"What if I leave?" she asked. "Won't they find me? Like you said at the club, if you could find me... then they might find me."

His dark eyes bored into hers. "Dante Marquez and Franco Delgado you mean?"

She flinched at the names of the Mafioso guys that were most likely trying to track down her whereabouts at this very moment. The ones that she had betrayed. She nodded.

"They won't find you here. Niccolo DeLuca is an old friend of mine. You've heard his name before?"

Claudia nodded slowly, her eyes wide. She had heard the name of the Italian whispered in tones of awe and fear by her former boyfriend and many of his crew. Though she had never laid eyes on the man, she knew he was a powerful person.

Tyson continued. "I've already discussed the matter with him and assured him that Dante's *ex-girlfriend*, the bird who flew the nest with information that should never have been found, has no interest in his affairs. Nic is in the process of severing his Miami connection, which will take care of Dante. As for the other, he may think he's all powerful in his Vegas tower, but he's a bug that can be crushed if need be." His voice was meant to be reassuring, but the way he spoke told her what she already knew: she was way over her head in his world.

Her mind worked furiously. "If this... Niccolo DeLuca is taking care of Dante, does that mean I'm safe? I can leave, I don't have to stay here."

"Claudia, you seem to be under the misunderstanding that you'll be leaving my home, which is most definitely not the case. Now that I have you here, you won't be leaving."

"You can't just decide to keep me here against my will," she gasped, her green eyes snapping. "That's kidnapping, asshole!"

He grinned at her, white teeth flashing in his face. "How can it be kidnapping when you don't actually exist, Claudia Cantore? You're an illegal immigrant living under an assumed name. You've basically given me the means to take you, no strings attached."

Fury sparkled in her eyes, the whisky warming her veins giving her courage. "I'll call the Canadian consulate, they'll have you arrested for this. My testimony against Franco, Dante and this Niccolo DeLuca should ensure my safe passage back to Canada."

Reaching out, Tyson plucked the empty glass from her fingers before she decided to do something stupid with it, like smash it against his skull. "You were too smart to go to the feds before. We both know that's an empty threat. Baby, if you went with your information to the authorities now, you wouldn't last one night without my protection. There's no one that can protect you from the guys that are looking for you, except me. It's time to stop fighting the inevitable."

"I haven't even started fighting yet," she snarled, slapping her hands against his shoulders and shoving with all her strength. He didn't move an inch, only stared at her, drinking in the incredible beauty of her anger.

He let her push until she realized there was no moving him and cringed back into the plush couch as far as she could go. "Let. Me. GO!" she yelled in his face, emphasizing each word.

"That's not going to happen Claudia."

"Fuck you, Tyson King," she snapped.

"Enough," he growled. "Settle down."

"It's not enough, you fucking mobbed up asshole," she snarled at him, anger finally eclipsing her fear. "How dare you walk into my life like you somehow own me. I didn't let Dante get away with that shit and I sure as hell am not letting you do it. I will not stay here with you for a minute longer. I don't for a second believe that I'm in as much trouble as you say."

She dove under the arm that had her trapped against the couch and kicked out at his legs blindly hoping maybe she could get him in the crotch. A grunt of pain greeted her effort as her heel struck his thigh. She tried to wiggle across the couch, counting on the bruised thigh to slow him down a few seconds. He was faster than she thought possible considering his bulk. His hands clamped down on her and forced her face down into the couch where she had been trying to crawl away. He was on top of her in seconds, crushing her into the cushions.

The waft of cigar smoke from his shirt and the leather

scent of the couch filled her head as she gasped for air. Pinned underneath him, she couldn't move an inch. She yelled in protest when he leaned back, straddling her hips and reached for her arms, pinning them over her head. She struggled in his strong hold, only managing to wiggle her hips against him. He grunted in response, his hips rocking forward to thrust his erection against her backside, as if he couldn't help himself. Claudia froze.

"Good girl," he mumbled. "Hold still and I may be able to refrain from fucking you right here on the couch."

Claudia moaned, caught between wanting to struggle against his hold and knowing if she did she would likely end up getting herself into worse trouble. Her head was turned to the side, away from the couch. "Let me the fuck up," she managed to gasp. When his fingers only tightened on her wrists she cried out, "Please, just let me go!"

Tyson held her that way for a moment as if considering her plea. She knew what his answer would be, but it was still devastating when it came. "I won't let you go Claudia, not now that I have you."

"I hate you!" she cried out weakly.

He used his free hand to brush long strands of blond hair away from her face. "Maybe you do, and maybe you won't enjoy your stay here with me. I can promise you, Claudia, the more you fight this the less satisfied you'll be. As I said, I'm not a good man. I'll break you, if you give me no choice. But you'll live, which is more than I can say if you leave my protection."

She remained silent for a minute, digesting his words, then asked, "What do you want with me Tyson?"

He didn't answer her at first. Instead, he swept the hair off her neck and kissed the soft skin there, dragging his lips across her shoulder then back, following a path up the back of her neck and across to her ear. Her breath strangled in her throat and she let out a tiny moan as his lips whispered across the delicate shell of her ear. His tongue flicked out, tracing the nuances of her small ear, licking a fiery path back down to her neck. He lightly grazed his teeth across the skin, causing goosebumps to rise in his wake.

The gentle tenderness of his assault combined with the effects of the whisky caused a spike of pleasure to pass through her body from her ear down to her breasts, which were crushed into the couch, and further to her pussy, which responded with wet heat. She bit her cheek to stop a moan from escaping her lips. She swore at her traitorous body and demanded it stop responding to the giant kidnapping asshole holding her down. But her body continued to react as he kissed his way across the upper part of her bare back. He tilted his hips forward, pressing his erection into her ass again, branding her with the heat of his body.

His voice was deep and firm when he finally answered her, moving up her body again to speak in her ear, his big chest pressed against her back. "I want you in my life Claudia. I want to keep that beautiful smile I saw at the bank to myself. I want you living in my home, where I know no other man will be able to touch you again. But most of all, I want your gorgeous body in my bed, where I can fuck you whenever and however I want. I want to make you scream out loud as I take every part of you for myself."

CHAPTER FOUR

"Oh god," Claudia whimpered.

Tyson felt the tension thrumming through her body despite his much heavier one crushing her into the couch. He knew she was aroused, but fear threatened to overwhelm the desire she was beginning to feel. He had to remind himself to go slower with her. She wasn't some woman he picked up off the street for a quick fuck. For his purposes, she was pretty much an innocent in his world. Caught up in a drama she couldn't hope to cope with alone.

He eased his hips away from hers. If he thrust against her ass again he was likely to lose what little restraint he had left, shove her dress up the few inches it would take to get at her pussy and fuck her until she couldn't stand, let alone contemplate leaving his penthouse without permission and an armed escort.

"Calm down, baby. I'm not trying to scare you."

"Then why did you say that... that you want to keep me and have... sex with me?" she whispered, her voice shaking.

He sighed and released his grip on her wrists. He felt something like remorse when he saw the red marks marring her white skin. It had been a very long time, if ever, that he'd needed to keep his strength in mind when dealing with a woman. He tended to pick tough women, whores with padded curves that could handle his appetites in the bedroom.

"I want truth between us. You asked me a question and I answered you honestly." He sat back, giving her room to roll onto her side, curl her legs up and bring her arms down. She wrapped them around her middle, as though protecting herself in some small way. He found himself fascinated with everything about her, including the way she moved, delicate and feminine. "You may not like what I have to say, but you'll always know I'm telling it like it is between us."

She lay on her side for another moment just breathing, then nodded in acknowledgement. "I guess I can appreciate that," she said softly, pushing herself up until she was sitting once more. She shoved her hair back off of her face, the honeyed ends feathering around her in disarray.

Tyson watched her movements, mesmerized. No matter how she ended up in his penthouse, he couldn't regret bringing her here, even if it was under duress. He had wanted her badly, had men watching her every movement, and had studied pictures of her daily. He had absorbed every word of the information collected on her until it was memorized: height, weight, family, birth origins, birth name, alias, education, jobs, sexual partners. The last part had made him want to commit murder. It was also the knowledge that he could cheerfully kill her ex lovers with his bare hands that convinced him his obsession with her was real and long term.

She looked at him, her green eyes large in her face. "You won't let me go?" she asked, as though needing to hear it out loud again.

"I won't let you go," he confirmed. "I can't let you go now. Delgado will have people out there waiting for you. I have enemies too, they would have noticed you leaving the club with me and sold the information."

She frowned. "Because of you I'm in danger again. You've given away my whereabouts. I was doing just fine before you came along."

He studied her features. "You were happy hiding in the shadows, working night shifts, barely seeing the light of day? So afraid that you would be tracked down that you broke from your family and friends and hid from the world? I also know that your boss at the café offered you partnership and you turned her down. Dante Marquez would have tracked you down eventually. He was already closing in when I first checked into your background. I more than likely saved your life. Now you have the necessary protection, rather than facing that conscienceless bastard alone."

She stared at him, her eyebrows raised. "Do you have any idea how arrogant that sounds? It's *your* conscience I'm questioning at the moment."

"Baby, you aren't raped and dead," he pointed out harshly, running his huge hands across short hair. "A certain amount of arrogance is required in my line of work. If I didn't believe in my own authority, no one else would either."

She appeared to mull this over. She seemed to subconsciously relax, loosening the arms she had wrapped around her waist. "What exactly do you do?"

He shrugged. "I have stakes in several lucrative businesses, a few casinos in Reno and one in Vegas, restaurant chains and clothing brands. I also acquire majority shares in struggling companies, have my team of consultants pull them out of the red then sell off what's left."

"That doesn't sound nice," she said. "Don't people lose their jobs that way?"

"If I didn't buy out the companies and fix them, they

would be snapped up by someone else or go under, in which case the staff of said company would lose their jobs anyway."

She continued to frown at him, her delicate brows arching downward in displeasure. "You aren't telling me everything, are you?" she asked intuitively. "You didn't obtain this kind of wealth just from buying and selling other companies. Unless you own Google or something."

Tyson knew from studying her that she had a sharp brain, except when it came to choosing lovers. He wasn't quite ready to enlighten her as to all of his business interests yet. "No, I don't own Google."

She stared at him. He could see her mind working. She wanted to know how far to push, how many questions he would let her have before shutting the conversation down. She was testing the boundaries of his supposed honesty. He couldn't blame her, but he was soon going to have to show her the error of using her inquisitive mind against him. He didn't need to be a mind reader to know what she was thinking.

"What then?" she demanded, taking that step over the line. "Do you also own illegal businesses? Is that how you've become so rich?"

"Claudia," he said her name warningly.

She persisted. "At a guess, I would say very few people in this country could afford private elevators and garages on the top of exclusive downtown high rises."

"You won't like the answers, Claudia, so stop asking the questions."

"Why should I?" she snapped, her tone sharp but also shaky with nerves. "You know everything there is to know about me. What are you hiding? Is it because you aren't a legitimate businessman? I want to know exactly who my kidnapper is and what he does for a living."

"Why do you want to know?" he asked quietly.

She didn't heed his dangerous tone, plunging on recklessly,

as though testing the limits of his patience as well as honesty. "I want to testify against you too, when I get free. I want to be able to tell the FBI all about you and your dirty businesses so they can nail you for that as well as unlawful confinement, you son-of-a-bitch."

The curse was barely out of her mouth when he reached across the length of the couch, grabbed her by the arms and dragged her struggling into his lap.

"Take your hands off me!" she shouted.

He picked her up like she weighed little more than a doll and forced her facedown across his lap. She tried to brace herself against the couch and push back off his lap, but he held her down easily with one huge hand spread across her back. With the other hand he yanked up the skirt of her dress, shoving it easily over her rounded ass.

The sight of her generous ass cheeks displayed in white lace panties nearly neutralized his previous anger. But he had to show her that she needed to be more careful when choosing her words. He didn't mind her anger, but she needed to learn how to control herself around him. The very few people who spoke to him the way she had tonight had immediately regretted what was left of their very short lives. Tyson hadn't reached his level of power by taking shit from anyone.

He wasn't about to allow his woman to think she could get away with bad behaviour. He had to ensure she knew what to expect from him from the start. Which meant she would learn to watch her tongue or take the beating he would mete out. He brought his hand down heavily across her buttocks. She shrieked at the painful contact and squirmed.

His dick responded instantly. "If you keep moving like that, I'm not going to wait to get you to my bed. I'm going to put you down on your hands and knees and fuck you right here."

She froze, her breaths coming out in shallow gasps.

Tyson spanked her ass several more times, taking pleasure in the sight of his mahogany skin against the creamy pink blush of hers. Her thighs and ass cheeks turned from pretty pink to red as he continued beating her backside. He loved the way her plump, resilient ass jumped under each blow from his hand. He had meant to discipline her, but found himself thoroughly enjoying each smack and the viewing feast it gave him.

He spanked her for longer than he had intended, his anger long since forgotten in the heat of his arousal. It was everything he could do not to thrust his hips up into her belly with each blow of his hand. She had to feel the brand of his hard cock against her. Finally he stopped, leaving his palm curved across the cheek of her ass.

His harsh, roughened breathing mingled with her quick gasps. She no longer struggled to get up; her body lay limp across his thighs. Her head was tilted away from him, her face not entirely visible. He wanted to see her expression, see if he had hurt her too much or if she was now more resigned to staying with him.

His eyes swept across her skin, noticing the pink flush that spread across her entire body from the one cheek he could see, down her neck, across her back and arms. The heat from her body seeped through his trousers, calling to him. He didn't think she was in so much pain that she couldn't move. He was beginning to realize she was turned on. So much so that it likely shocked her, paralyzing her.

There was only one way to find out. Pressing down on the middle of her back to keep her from arching up when she realized what he was doing, he ran the fingers of his other hand down the seam of her ass and pressed them firmly against her panty covered pussy. Satisfaction filled him when the rough pads of his fingers encountered hot, soaked lace. She was wet for him.

As he had anticipated, the intimate touch caused her to abandon her frozen state. She shouted something incoherent and tried to shove back against his restraining hand. Leaning forward, he covered her body with his chest, immobilizing her. He let her struggle until she realized she wasn't going anywhere.

"Are you done?" he asked, when she stopped moving.

She nodded her head. "Yes, yes!" she gasped. "Please, just let me go."

She sounded so near tears that Tyson decided to give her a little space, if that's what she needed. He eased up and let her slide off his lap, onto the floor. She kneeled in front of him with her skirt hiked up to her waist, and glared at him through wet, spiked lashes. Black mascara smudged under her eyes and ran down her cheeks. He reached out to wipe the black streak off her face. She jerked away from him, but he caught her arm and pulled her closer, between his spread knees.

Pressing his thumb against the skin of her cheek, he wiped the mark from her face. His hungry gaze took in her disheveled state. "So fucking beautiful. I have to have you in my bed tonight."

She stared at him, her eyes huge. "What if I say no?"

"Not an option."

Anger made the green of her eyes sparkle. "Or what? You'll toss me out onto the street where Franco Delgado can get me? Is that the alternative you're threatening me with?"

Tyson tightened his fingers on her arm, starting to weary of her constant denials. He was willing to give her some slack given her former independence, but he wouldn't allow her much. Especially not with the state of his cock, which was urging him to get on with things.

"I've told you my position Claudia, you aren't going anywhere. Not to Delgado and not to the feds. Hell, you won't even be going for a walk around the block without my permission. It's time to stop the dramatics and just accept things as is. I've created a situation in which the only safe place for you is here in my penthouse, which includes my bed. There is no choice here."

"You'd rape me?" she whispered.

His Claudia was as forthright as her profile had described her. He didn't care to dance around subjects either, nor did he want to frighten her unnecessarily. But if she demanded the truth then he would give it to her. "That's up to you, baby. You enjoy my touch. Your body reacts to me as though made for mine. I can make our sexual encounters entirely enjoyable for you if you let me."

She swallowed, her throat moving nervously. "And if I don't?"

"Then I'll just have to spank you until you do."

She stared at him, her brain rapidly trying to come to some kind of solution. She clearly didn't want to give in to him. Not because she didn't desire him (she very much did at that moment), but because her strong, independent mind couldn't imagine submitting to him in any way. Most certainly not sexually. Yet she knew there were no other options. She couldn't physically best him and he wasn't about to let her look for a way to escape, as he had no doubt she would start searching for the moment he was out of her sight.

Licking her lips, her gaze slid away from his. "Can I please clean up? Do you have a washroom I can use?"

Her clever mind found the only other option. Delay the inevitable and appeal to his sense of humanity.

"Yes," he said, standing. She immediately scooted backward so he wouldn't touch her. He reached a hand out to her, which she took after some hesitation.

He helped her stand and waited while she tugged her dress back down over her hips. Then, still holding her hand, he led her through the living room, past the kitchen and down the hall toward the bedrooms. She tried to stop in front of the main floor washroom, but he refused to release her, pulling her toward a set of stairs leading up to the second floor of his penthouse.

"Where are you taking me?" she asked sharply, afraid he intended to take her to bed right away.

"I want you in my space. You can use my private washroom."

She relaxed a little and allowed him to pull her up the stairs. She gasped in appreciation when they stepped into his bedroom, which took up most of the top floor and was surrounded by windows. She spun around on the spot staring out into the city, lit up with twinkling lights. Forgetting about her predicament for the moment, she walked to the window and pressed her hands against the glass.

"I've never seen anything so beautiful," she whispered in awe.

Tyson approached her, enjoying the sight of her in his bedroom. He wanted her naked and sprawled out on his bed, a huge king plus that sat on a platform and dominated one corner of the room, but he was willing to wait a few more minutes if it meant letting her become more comfortable. He kneeled on the plush carpet next to her feet. She didn't notice until he reached down and pressed one hand against the back of her knee while the other lifted her ankle. She gasped and swayed, pressing her palm more firmly against the glass window so she wouldn't fall. He slid her high heel off.

Leaning forward he did the same with her other shoe. She was stiff with apprehension, but she didn't try to back away from his firm touch. He placed her barefoot on the floor, watching as her toes curled into the soft carpet. Her tiny toenails were painted bright pink. He wanted to lick her toes and feel them curl against his tongue the way they did in the carpet.

His face was so close to her hips that when he breathed in he could smell the sweet, spicy aroma of her cunt mixed with the odour of vanilla lotion. He had to dig his fingers into his thighs to keep from dragging her down into the carpet and tearing her clothes off. Instead, he stood up, towering over her and gestured to the only side of the room without windows.

"The ensuite," he said, taking her hand and guiding her toward the door.

He flipped the light on, illuminating a modern facility with a shower and huge sunken tub as well as a marble vanity with dual sinks. The other side of the ensuite led through to a massive walk in closet that took up the rest of the second floor. She stared around for a moment, dazed.

Finally she tilted her head and looked up at him. "Can't I use the washroom downstairs?"

"No," he responded immediately. "I've told you how things will be between us, Claudia. Start getting used to it. I'll give you some extra time if you decide you want to take a shower." He indicated the shadowy doorway that led to his closet. "Back there you can find my clothes if you wish to change. They'll be too big, but they'll have to do until we can arrange a wardrobe for you. I'll send Daniel over to your place tomorrow to pick up some things."

"Awesome," she snapped. "So you're going to kidnap my stuff as well as me? That's really great."

Tyson pulled her around to face him. Reaching out he took hold of her jaw and tilted her face up. In a controlled voice, he said, "Don't test my patience too far Claudia, it's not unlimited. In fact, I've never been known for my abundant tolerance, but I'm trying with you."

She jerked her chin out of his hand and stepped away

from him. He allowed her to break his hold on her arm. She crossed her arms over her breasts, pushing them up in a way he enjoyed. "You could have fooled me. If this is you being patient then you need some lessons buddy."

Tyson stared down at her for a moment and then laughed, his deep voice booming. Surprised, she jumped back. He shook his head, grinning. "I have absolutely no doubt you'll be teaching me patience by trial woman. Let's hope you survive the lessons."

With that he turned and left her alone, closing the door firmly behind him. He would go downstairs and set the alarm and see about getting her something to eat for later. For now, she could be alone to contemplate her future with him. Hopefully she would somehow come to terms with things. He really didn't want to hurt her, but he feared it might be inevitable. She was unpredictable and had an explosive, quick temper.

CHAPTER FIVE

C laudia took two minutes to use the toilet and wash her
hands. She placed her hands on the vanity and stared
at herself in the mirror. She hated the vulnerable, frightened
look in her green eyes. She'd been running for more than a
year, with the threat of Dante and Franco Delgado always
close behind. After arranging for fake ID and stealing information that would incriminate Franco Delgado's illegal business in Vegas and Dante Marquez's in Miami, she had fled.
She'd also paid a hacker to arrange for fake records for her
fake ID. For six months, she had run from state to state,
never settling down. Unable to cope with a nomadic lifestyle,
she finally took a risk and set herself up here, in Tyson King's
city. After eight months, the fear of discovery had finally
started to fade.

She breathed deeply, urging her heart to slow down and
her brain to start moving faster. She couldn't have her wits
scattered if she was going to get out of this new mess. Staying
with Tyson King was not an option. She would find a way out
of his penthouse and then she'd leave the city. Go on the run

again. Then, maybe find a way to contact her family in Canada.

She missed them. Her break from them had been painful. They hadn't understood how their daughter, a woman who had always been successful and kind, could have been sucked into the Vegas lifestyle and thrust them away so callously. She hadn't dared contact them in more than a year, which led them to fear their only child was dead, a victim of the scene she had willingly become a part of when she moved to Las Vegas to become a showgirl.

The first thing Claudia had to do was find a weapon. She didn't stand a chance against Tyson if he caught her. His giant, muscular frame could too easily subdue her. She searched the drawers in the washroom and came up with nothing. No aerosol cans she could use to spray him in the face, no conveniently hidden knives, nothing. Next, she checked the massive walk in closet, tossing clothes and shoes on the floor in her haste.

The best she could come up with was a box filled with tie pins. She picked the longest one she could find. It was made out of gold and about the length of her finger with a sharp tip. It wouldn't cause much damage, but with luck she'd be able to find her way out without running into anyone.

Claudia opened the washroom door and glanced around the empty bedroom. She felt fairy certain Tyson went downstairs. She briefly considered putting her heels back on, but decided they would slow her down. Forcing herself to think without panicking she tried to decide how to get out of the penthouse. It wasn't going to be easy.

She had seen a door on the first level that led outside to what she assumed was a balcony. A man with Tyson's wealth likely had a heated pool out there. There would also maybe be another exit that way, but chances were it was going to be locked.

Think, Claudia!

She could come up with nothing that involved staying safely away from Tyson. She would have to somehow get past him and into the lobby. If the elevators were locked, as she suspected they were, since he wouldn't want just anyone accessing his penthouse, she would then have to get into the garage. Maybe she could find a set of keys, get into one of the cars and somehow figure out how to get that car elevator to work.

And maybe a flying unicorn would come rescue her.

But she had to try.

Claudia made her way down the spiral staircase as silently as she could. It was made out of wood flooring, like the main floor. Her bare feet whispered against the hardwood as she moved cautiously. She heard voices as she made her way onto the main level of the penthouse. Her heart sped up. Did he have someone with him?

As she made her way down the hall, hugging the wall, she realized it was music. Soft jazz instrumentals filled the space. She also heard him moving around the kitchen, like he was cooking. It seemed odd to her that a man with his kind of wealth might cook for himself when he could probably afford to have a five star chef on staff. Not that she cared. She wasn't going to be around long enough to see if he was any good.

Keeping to the shadows, she peeked around the corner. He was indeed working in the kitchen. His big, black forearms strained against the white dress shirt, rolled up to his elbows, as he cut into an avocado on a thick wooden cutting board. She stood frozen until he turned his back to her and opened the fridge. Claudia dove forward, crouching down behind the marble-topped island.

She held her breath, heart hammering in her chest. She thanked god the music masked her swift dash. The chopping noises resumed a few feet away from her head. Trying not to picture the sharp knife in his huge hand and how angry he would be when he found her missing, she started to creep forward, making sure she was covered by shadows.

She made it to the far side of the island and prayed he would need to open the fridge once more. A moment later she heard the promising suction sound of a fridge opening. She dove forward again, staying crouched and refusing to look back over her shoulder. She made it to the hallway leading to the front door and glided softly toward the big wooden door.

It was locked on the inside with a heavy duty deadbolt. But it wasn't the deadbolt that caught her attention, it was the alarm panel, flashing red with the words 'alarm set' that concerned her. Fuck. She would alert him and probably his security detail the moment she opened the door. She placed a hand on the deadbolt and considered her options. She could try to sneak back through the kitchen and pretend she was coming from upstairs. Or she could go into the kitchen, hand him the tie pin and apologize with the hope that he wouldn't be too angry.

Or she could take door number three – the stupidest option. She would open this door, set off the damn alarm and run faster than she'd ever run in her life to get to one of those cars. Maybe it would be unlocked with keys in it and a car elevator opener that was appropriately labeled.

And maybe the unicorn that came to rescue her would be rainbow coloured and shit gold bars.

Fuck it.

Claudia slammed the deadbolt back, opened the surprisingly heavy door and bolted into the elevator lobby. The alarm sounded immediately, spurring her to run faster as she pelted past the elevators. She hit the down button but didn't bother to stop for an elevator. She knew there would be a key or a code in order to get off or on the penthouse floor. She hoped, though, that she could trick Tyson and his men into thinking she had somehow locked herself in the elevator.

The glass doors leading into the garage weren't locked. She dragged the door open and rushed into the darkened interior. Behind her she heard the door to the apartment being wrenched open. Tyson was fast on his feet for such a big guy.

"Claudia, stop!" he thundered, staring at her through the glass. His face looked forbidding. He barely paused before charging forward.

Claudia knew her plan was doomed to fail from the outset, but she still turned and fled. She ran for the first SUV to her left and yanked on the door handle. Unlocked! It was her first stroke of luck. She dove inside, shut the door and slammed the lock down just as Tyson reached the vehicle. The look on his face when he tried the handle and found it locked was enough to convince Claudia she should probably spend the rest of her life inside. Because her odds on the outside were decidedly grim.

"Open it, Claudia," he growled, slamming his palm against the window, causing the entire vehicle to rock.

She ignored him and began searching for keys. She was relatively certain she wouldn't find any, but it gave her something to do besides look at the wrathful visage of her abductor. After a minute, she looked up and realized Tyson was no longer there. Frantically, she searched the garage, but he was definitely gone.

Then he was walking back toward her with purpose. She stared at him, terrified. The unmistakable click let her know he had disengaged the door locks with a key fob.

"No!"

She tried to crawl over the console to go out the other door, but he yanked open the drivers side door and grabbed her by the hair. He pulled her backwards, not exerting enough force to really hurt her, but she knew if she struggled he would make it hurt. He slammed the door shut once she was clear of the vehicle. He pulled her around until she was facing him. Without the four extra inches of height her heels had given her, she was much shorter than him. He stared down at her, his eyes glacial.

"I had to try," she whispered.

He shook his head. "You should have listened to me, Claudia."

The door to the garage banged open and Mercer, backed by two other men she didn't recognize, stalked into the garage. His hair was disheveled and he was wearing only jeans, no doubt awakened by the security alarm. He held a gun in his right hand so comfortably it looked like it was an extension of his arm. "Secure the garage," he snapped at the guys behind him.

Tyson let go of her hair, but took her firmly by the arm. He dragged her toward Mercer, stopping in front of the body-guard. "She set off the alarm when she ran for the garage," he said to Mercer. "Good response time. Make sure no one slipped through. I'll secure her for the night. This time I'll make sure she stays put."

Mercer nodded shortly, his icy eyes sweeping Claudia and the boss, checking for injuries.

Claudia might have ogled the insanely chiseled pectoral muscles and abs of Tyson's bodyguard if he wasn't such a cold-blooded monster and if she wasn't in the midst of being kidnapped. And if she weren't pretty sure it would get the other man killed by his boss. Suddenly she wished very much for Anya. Her friend, a healthy red-blooded woman with good eyesight, would understand her current dilemma.

Tyson pulled Claudia back toward the penthouse. "What does that mean? How will you secure me?" she asked, hurrying to keep up with his much longer strides. He clearly wasn't in the mood to slow down for her. Her bare feet hurried over the cold pavement as he forced her to go with him.

He ignored her question, dragging her through the lobby and back into the penthouse. He slammed the door shut, locked it and re-engaged the alarm. He finally let go of her arm. Claudia rubbed it where his fingers had bit into her skin. He stalked into the living room and turned to look at her.

"Come here."

Heart pounding, Claudia lifted her chin and walked toward him. She stopped about a foot away and stared back at him. Unable to handle his prolonged angry silence, she said, "I can't just stay here. You know I'm not willing to accept this situation as is."

"Damn it, Claudia," he said furiously. "You can't begin to comprehend how much danger you're in. You can be killed easily if you manage to leave my protection. That was a stupid thing to do, despite the fact that you wouldn't have made it out of the garage."

"I'm just supposed to take your word for it that I'm in danger?" she snapped back. "And if my life is in danger currently, that would be your fault for alerting the men that want me dead as to my whereabouts. I'm better off on my own than with an egotistical, kidnapping asshole!"

"Enough!" he snarled. "Stop talking, Claudia."

"Don't you dare tell me to stop..." he grabbed her so quickly she didn't have a chance to react. He pulled one of her wrists behind her back and held it tightly with one hand, while gripping her jaw in his other hand. Before she could protest, his mouth descended to hers, crushing her soft lips in a ruthless kiss.

She pushed helplessly against his chest, her fist slamming into him. He continued to punish her mouth, forcing her head back until her neck ached. He used his fingers to pry her jaw open and plundered the interior of her mouth, while holding her open so she couldn't bite. His tongue swept across hers, caressing her teeth and plunging deep, stealing her breath.

Tears pricked her eyes and, unable to breath, she began to sway against him. The kiss continued on and on until she thought she would pass out. Desperately, Claudia finally lashed out with the tie pin still held in her fist. She aimed the sharp point at his neck and jabbed him with it. It didn't penetrate his thick neck very far, but it startled him.

"What the fuck!" he snarled, immediately ending the kiss and reaching for the wound.

His hand came up to his neck so fast that Claudia didn't have time to duck. It struck her hard in the side of the head. Already off balance, she tumbled sideways, hitting the island hard and falling to the floor. She stayed where she landed, dazed and terrified of his retaliation.

Tyson realized right away what had happened when he pulled the pin out of his neck. He stared down at her, his face unreadable. She shrieked and backed into the island, pulling her knees up, when he crouched in front of her. He searched her pale face and then gently touched his fingers to the red mark on her cheek where he had struck her.

"I'm sorry, baby. I never meant to hurt you." His tone was regretful and his touch gentle.

Claudia was completely exhausted. She nodded slowly and forced her limbs to uncurl. "I know," she said. "I'm sorry I stabbed you. It was a bad plan from the beginning. Your neck is incredibly thick, like your head."

He laughed. "That tiny prick is definitely not a stabbing, beautiful. Believe me, I've seen plenty of bad shit in my life." He backed up and held a hand out to her. She took it with some hesitation and allowed him to pull her to her feet.

"Though, now that I know you're willing to use weapons against me, I'll have to increase my vigilance."

She smiled slightly. "I don't think I have the stomach for a real stabbing. I regretted pricking you almost as soon as I did it."

"If your life was ever in danger, I would expect you to use whatever weapons are at your disposal with deadly force." His face grew serious. "Never take a weapon to me again though, sweetheart. That sort of behaviour won't stand between us. I could have seriously injured you, even if it was an accident. You need to be more careful."

She arched a blond eyebrow at him. "Seriously? You're telling me to be careful around the hulking giant in case he accidentally, what... falls on me or something?"

"Funny," he said, urging her onto one of the barstools at the island. "I'm telling you not to prick me, stab me, burn me or whatever else that imagination can come up with. It may end in an injury to you, and I can't abide the idea."

His dark eyes held hers. She nodded slowly. It felt like a bizarre conversation to be having, but then again, she did stab him after trying to run away and steal one of his vehicles. So all told, she was getting off pretty lightly with just a forceful kiss and an accidental smack to the side of the head, which he apologized for. Strange man.

And now, it would appear that he was making her a sandwich. He toasted a couple pieces of focaccia bread, spread mayo on them and added turkey, tomato, lettuce and avocado. She salivated while he prepared the food for her and placed the sandwich in front of her.

"This is my favourite sandwich at Knight's Out, where I work. I eat them almost every day," she said, picking it up and taking a huge bite.

"I know," he said, watching her eat.

She stopped chewing and stared at him. He really did

know everything about her, right down to her food preferences. The thought should probably frighten her, since she barely knew the guy. But strangely, she felt cared for. Something she hadn't felt in a very long time. Tears prickled in the corners of her eyes, as longing for her parents swept over her. She dropped her gaze and took another healthy bite of the sandwich.

"What's going to happen to my job?" she asked once she had swallowed the food in her mouth.

"Don't worry about it. Your job's been taken care of."

She frowned at him. "And what exactly does that mean? I don't have a job anymore, or you arranged things so I could leave for a while?"

His eyes caught and held hers. "I mean, you can stop worrying about the café job. Your boss has been compensated for giving you a job in your time of need and recognizing your talent. However, she's aware that your services are no longer for sale."

Claudia's jaw dropped. "What in the actual hell!?" she snapped. "That's just great! Do you have any idea how freaking hard it is to get a job when you can't provide a criminal record check or references?"

Tyson sighed in annoyance and rubbed a hand over his head, "Just shut up and eat Claudia."

She seriously thought about arguing, but decided her empty stomach combined with his ridiculous misogynistic attitude made eating quietly more advisable. For the moment anyway.

He watched her finish her sandwich without further comment, his gaze lingering on her lips. He ate the leftover avocado and tomato from the cutting board and then began cleaning up. He was a very tidy man. Everything had a place. He definitely wasn't the type to toss a coat on the floor or let piles of paper stack up on a table or desk. Exactly the opposite of her. She had an armchair in her tiny apartment that was dedicated full-time to holding clothes. She used her treadmill as a drying rack for hang-to-dry clothes (once she discovered she hated running even more than washing clothes by hand) and she dedicated her pantry to shoes, since the shelves were a perfect fit and she despised cooking.

"Thank you," she said politely once she finished eating. She wiped her mouth on the napkin he handed her and then dropped it onto the plate, which he took.

After finishing up in the kitchen, he came around the island and pulled her stool back. "Time for bed," he said, putting a hand on her arm and helping her off the stool.

Claudia stood next to him, looking up well over half a foot. He was such a big man, she wondered if she would get used to his size. Then she blushed, remembering the size of his erection as it had pressed against her. Her heart picked up speed and her mouth went dry. She stumbled a little when he tugged her forward toward the stairs. He turned the stereo and lights out behind them as they left the room.

When they arrived upstairs he turned to look at her. The lights from the city created a gentle glow in the glass-walled room. He touched her face, running his fingers over her cheeks. "I want to fuck you more than I've ever wanted any other woman, Claudia."

She nodded, knowing he was going to have his way. At least, she hoped, he would make sure she enjoyed herself. She supposed she should feel grateful for that.

"But tonight, I think you just need sleep," he said, stepping back from her.

Her eyes flew up to his. "You're not going to..."

He chuckled, "Not now, baby. Believe me, I want nothing more than to fuck that delicious body. But I prefer my women conscious and you look as though you're seconds from passing out on me."

She had no idea how anxious she was about the inevitability of sharing his bed, but once he announced her reprieve, tension left her body. She closed her eyes in relief, tiredness overwhelming her. She swayed on the spot, unable to open her eyes again.

He reached for her before she could collapse.

"I've got you, sweetheart."

He laid her on the bed. Claudia drifted off to the feel of him removing her clothes from her limp body.

CHAPTER SIX

Tyson had meant to let her sleep. She had been so tired the evening before, she hadn't murmured a protest when he'd removed her clothes and settled her on his bed. He had also meant to put one of his T-shirts on her. Good intentions fled as her beautiful, curvaceous body was revealed to him. Careful not to disturb her, he reached over and turned a lamp on. Her skin glowed pale in the dim lighting of the room.

He wondered how this goddess hadn't been snapped up before now. She was perfection, from her long, slim feet to her wide hips, small waist, rounded breasts and graceful neck. She wasn't fashionably slim, but soft and curved in a way that made Tyson's mouth water.

Despite her incredible body, it was her face that arrested him most. Her thick eyelashes, slightly darker than her honey blond hair, were swept down across the top of her cheeks. Her eyes, which sparked green fire when she was angry or turned to shining liquid when she was turned on. She had a strong jaw and a wide mouth with full lips. He loved the feel of her plush lips under his.

He allowed her a few hours sleep before deciding he could wait no longer. He had patiently waited months to have her in his power, and now even a few hours longer felt like too many. Tyson always got what he wanted, and he wanted Claudia.

His plan was to make sure she was well and truly turned on before taking her. He was not a small man, and though she wasn't exactly small either, he knew very few women could take him comfortably on the first encounter. Especially a woman of Claudia's relative inexperience. She'd had few lovers in her twenty-nine years and none in the last fourteen months. The wetter she was for him, the better it would be for her.

He didn't want to wake her up right away, as he was fairly certain she would begin struggling. He disliked the thought of coercing her consent. Though he would, if necessary. He would do what was required to bring Claudia under his power. But for some reason the thought of hurting Claudia more than he already had wasn't particularly palatable to him.

He started with light touches, sweeping a hand down her body, gliding over her silken skin. She didn't move. Growing more bold, he lingered over her breasts and hips. Touching her as she slept. His mouth watered at the thought of tasting her. Never one to deny himself, Tyson leaned over and gently took the peak of one plump breast into his mouth. He swept his tongue across and around the pink nipple, enjoying the way she sighed and shifted slightly toward his hot mouth. The peak stiffened in his mouth, encouraging him to move onto her other breast to administer similar treatment.

Claudia shifted restlessly on the bed, her naked body sliding against the sheets. She looked like a goddess in the glow of the lamp, with the gorgeous waves of her hair spread across his dark bedding. He sifted the fingers of one hand through the powdery soft strands, marvelling at the delicate look of the locks against his big, dark hand. His cock surged at the sinful sight, urging him to continue with his seductive intentions.

Tyson was a big man. There was no getting around the physics of their differing body sizes. He wanted her to enjoy their coupling, but worried he might hurt her. He had wanted her so badly for so long that he was afraid once he started, he wouldn't be able to go slow enough for her to adjust.

He knew her body wasn't as used to penetration as he would have liked. Not that he wanted to imagine her with other guys, but the thought of her playing with sex toys had him vowing to do a little online shopping once she was over her initial shyness. Which is something he would spend the next several weeks working on. Tyson had never been an inhibited man and he suspected Claudia could match his sexual appetites once she felt truly freed from the stresses of the past few years. He acknowledged that her existence was one of survival with little time for sexual awareness. He relished the thought of remedying that.

He knew from their earlier tussle on the couch that she was capable of passion with him. That she had been turned on was undeniable, despite her resistance. He knew he could make sex good for her and he looked forward to bringing her pleasure more than any multi-million dollar acquisition. Glad that she continued to sleep deeply, he eased the blankets and sheets that had tangled around her hips and legs away from her body. She murmured a tiny protest and mindlessly reached for the disappearing warmth.

Tyson took her wrist in his hand and gently held it against the bed until she settled again. He let her go and very gently pressed her legs apart. She had a thatch of honey blond hair protecting her vagina. She had shaved around the lips and clitoris though. He had always enjoyed a natural look on women, but found he also liked being able to see every pink part of her. He eased his body in between her legs, mindful of spreading them too much and waking her with his shoulders wedged in between her thighs.

He spread one hand above her pussy across her lower abdomen, enjoying the contrast in skin colour. The soft curve of her belly felt so good against his roughened fingers. He slid his hand forward, gently touching the light-coloured pubic hair curled above the part of her he craved to taste. He used the fingers of both hands to spread her labia apart and examine the tiny hooded clitoris nestled within. Softly, he petted her inner lips and clitoris with one big finger, shaking slightly at the effort it took not to devour her in an instant.

Tyson knew that, in order to play his cards right, she would have to be mindless with lust before she woke up and before he forced her body to take his huge cock. He was not normally known for his consideration of others, but Claudia was different. Though, through his heavy-handed intervention, she was now living in his home, he wanted her to be happy. If he could satisfy her sexually, she may learn to enjoy her time with him. He realized now that her body was only one facet of what he wanted. He also wanted to own her smiles, her happiness and her joy. He wanted every part of her.

A better man might have given her more time to adjust to life with him before making sexual demands. Tyson was used to getting what he wanted, and he was done waiting to have his woman. Leaning forward, he flicked his tongue over her clit. She quivered, but didn't wake up. He stroked her with his tongue, learning every part of how she felt and tasted. He took his time, stroking her at leisure, prolonging the moment of her waking.

His hand shook with need as he gripped her thigh and gently pushed it back, giving him better access to the heart of her. He gently pressed a thick finger into the sweet folds of her vagina, entering her slowly and savouring the tight clasp. She was wet enough to ease his way, but she was still incredibly tight. He stroked his tongue up her labia and sucked on her clit, drawing the tiny bud out.

Claudia moaned and shifted in her sleep. She rocked her hips forward, pressing her pussy against the tongue that was pleasuring her so well. She tossed her head and brought one delicate hand up to clasp her pillow.

Tyson continued to arouse her body, enjoying the beautiful pink flush that was spreading out from her core. He knew that she would wake soon and pressed his advantage, sucking and licking her with more force. He pressed his finger in and out of her body, her own pleasure easing his way. He added another finger, gently stretching her.

With a moan and a gasp, Claudia woke up.

"Tyson?" she asked, her voice husky with sleep. She blinked down her pale body at him.

He tensed, expecting fear or anger.

Claudia frowned and shifted her legs restlessly. She tried to close them, but his wide shoulders, wedged between her thighs, stopped her. The heels of her slender feet brushed against his biceps. She stared at him, her eyes wide and cloudy. Tyson moved his fingers out of her body and thrust them back in, pressing the pads of his fingers against her g-spot as he slid home. She cried out and arched her neck back, widening her thighs.

Tyson hadn't realized that she was so close to orgasm. He'd thought only to pleasure her and then convince her to go further when she woke up. He hadn't imagined she would be this responsive. She rocked her hips back and forth against his fingers, encouraging him to continue thrusting into her willing body. Tyson obliged and lowered his face to continue his oral assault.

"Oh god!" she moaned, reaching down to place a hand on the back of his head, her fingers grazing his thick hair.

Tyson grinned and around the delicious folds of her pussy said, "That's Tyson to you, darling."

"Tyson, Tyson!" she called out as his tongue drove her relentlessly toward the precipice of her orgasm.

She screamed, her body shaking and bucking against him as she came. Tyson gripped her legs tightly and watched as the most beautiful woman he could imagine flew apart in ecstasy. He had known for months that this obsession with Claudia Cantore was more than fleeting. Now he knew for sure. He was in love with the woman. He wanted all of her smiles, all of her words and all of her orgasms. He was keeping her forever.

Kneeling above her, Tyson reached for a condom and rolled it on over a cock that was almost painfully erect. He watched as she drifted back down from the high of her orgasm, a blush spreading across her breasts and the peaks of her stiff little nipples. He watched as she realized what was about to happen and slowly turned her head on the pillow, her soft, pale hair a halo against the dark sheets.

"Tyson..." she whispered.

"I'm going to fuck you now, baby," he said, gripping her thighs in his hands and forcing her legs back, exposing her lush pussy. "You will belong to me after tonight."

―――――――――

A pleasurable buzz flowed through Claudia's body. Her head was fuzzy from sleep and the remnants of her orgasm. She couldn't think, couldn't piece together what was happening to her. All she knew was she wanted Tyson's long, thick cock inside her. She shivered when he shoved her legs back, rendering her helpless. She gripped the pillows in her hands and rocked her hips against the smooth sheets.

She watched him as he looked down at her exposed pussy. He stroked a finger tenderly through the slippery folds, then took his cock in hand and lined it up against her vagina. Claudia knew it would hurt. It had been a long time since she'd been with a man. Not since Dante. When she masturbated, she used only finger to clit contact, rarely fingering herself inside.

"This might hurt, baby," Tyson grunted, pressing the tip forward.

Claudia thrust her hips up to meet him, grinding her teeth against the pressure as he penetrated her. "You... flatter yourself!" she gasped out.

Tyson's laugh rumbled down his chest and against her legs. Claudia cried out as pressure turned to pain. Then he wasn't laughing anymore. He held himself still, the tendons on his neck straining as he held himself tightly in check. Sweat beaded his dark forehead.

Claudia forced herself to relax under him, the pressure of his entry gradually diminishing. Tyson dropped his head and kissed her leg close to where his hands gripped.

"That's a good girl," he grunted.

He pushed himself steadily further into her resisting body until he was completely engulfed by the heat of her pussy. He waited until she once more relaxed before pulling back. Like a dance, he moved forward within her and then withdrew, using her body language to gauge when he should thrust or retreat. She took him beautifully, bravely moving her hips up to meet his, seeking her own pleasure once more.

Claudia was more than a match for any man in bed. She was passionate and loved the pleasure she could find in sex. Tyson was more than she had ever had in her bed before. He was generous, he was demanding and he was huge. She couldn't deny him. She didn't want to. She wanted the big, dark-skinned man to fuck her until she lost herself once more in the oblivion of orgasm.

Reaching up, Claudia clasped her hands behind his neck and forced his head down to hers. "Fuck me like you mean it," she said and took his lips in a passionate kiss, thrusting her tongue into his mouth.

The tensing of his shoulders was the only warning she got. His tongue met hers and shoved back. His hands fell to her hips and he gripped her tightly, slamming himself up into her. Claudia gasped, her head falling back. She reached up and gripped the sheets and pillows above her head. Tyson thrust into her with such force that she was pushed up the bed. He dragged her back down and held her still while he impaled her body with ferocious intent.

Claudia cried out and moaned, unable to do anything but hang on. He slammed her hips down, fucking into her over and over again. The way he tilted her hips shoved the head of his penis against her g-spot, pushing her higher and higher than she'd ever been before. Without warning, Claudia found herself pushed over the edge of another, more intense orgasm.

He picked her hips right up off the bed, his thrusts growing deeper and more erratic. With a shout he came, bringing her hips down onto his cock in one last brutal thrust. He moved his hands from her hips to her waist and picked her right up, bringing her upper body into the cradle of his arms. He tilted her face so he could watch her as they drifted down together.

Claudia collapsed against him, pressing her cheek against the muscles of his chest. The heavy beat of his heart sounded against her ear. She snuggled into his warmth, letting him hold her up. She felt the rumble in his body as he chuckled and dropped a kiss against the top of her head. She wanted to deny it, but she had never in her life felt safer than in that moment.

Claudia listened as his heartbeat gradually calmed. After a minute, he lifted her off of his cock, ignoring her murmur of protest. He laid her on the bed with such care that she imagined she was more precious to him in that moment than anything else in the world. He stood up and went into the washroom. Claudia was already drifting back into sleep when she felt the bed dip under his big body as he kneeled on the bed.

He brushed the hair off her cheek and tucked it behind her ear. Claudia forced her eyes open and looked up at him. His eyes reflected triumph, which would have annoyed her more if she weren't so satisfied herself.

"Don't think this changes anything," she said with a yawn. "I'm still upset about this kidnapping bullshit. Just because you're some kind of sexual god doesn't mean I won't kick your ass in the morning."

He flashed her a white-toothed grin. "I look forward to the battle, beautiful."

"Then you better get some sleep so I don't beat you up too badly." She slid a hand up his arm and tried to tug him down beside her.

Tyson reached behind him and turned the lamp off before allowing himself to be pulled down into her arms. She snuggled into the warmth of the bed, enjoying the feeling of sleeping safe for the first time in a long time – at the top of Tyson King's tower. In the morning she would contemplate this new turn her life had taken and what her next steps would be.

CHAPTER SEVEN

Claudia sat on the bed, her legs tucked underneath her in a prim pose, wearing only a button-up shirt. She rebelled against the stereotype of wearing one of her lover's shirts, but it was this or her blue dress. She had tried on Tyson's bathrobe and it had engulfed her to the point that she felt like a three year-old playing dress up. She had gotten one of the sleeves thoroughly soaked when she'd tried to wash her hands. She had hung it back up and moved on to Tyson's shirts. Still irked about her forceful relocation, she had chosen one that looked decidedly expensive.

Now, she sat luxuriating in the lovely feel of the fabric against her bare skin and watched Tyson sleep. He really was a giant of a man. With the morning light shining in the windows, her eyes could trace over the long limbs of his legs and arms sprawled carelessly across the sheets. His middle parts had been uncovered too. His penis, even soft, was long and imposing. She had flicked the sheet over that part of his anatomy before continuing her inspection. She squirmed a bit, her body sore, reminding her of the way he had so thoroughly taken her the night before.

She placed a hand on his chest, feeling the rise and fall against her palm. She studied their skin, fascinated by the difference in their skin colours. She had never particularly considered men beautiful, but Tyson held an appeal that was new to her. His skin was incredibly dark next to hers. It was smooth to touch. Soft, but also hard where her fingers skimmed over muscle. Even the scars that puckered parts of his chest, arm and neck seemed somehow different against his dark skin.

Fingers seized her hand, pressing it flat against his chest. Claudia gasped, her eyes flying to his. He was watching her, his face serious and intent. She blushed and tried to pull her hand away, but he held her tight. When she stopped trying to pull away, he reached up, took hold of her shoulders and pulled her down on top of him. His lips sought hers and he stole an unexpectedly chaste kiss before releasing her.

Claudia pushed off of him and sat back up, scooting back out of reach of his long arms. He grinned and stretched his arms behind his head. His eyes devoured her, taking in her attire and long bare legs.

"You look beautiful in the morning," he announced.

Claudia snorted. "I look like Oscar the Grouch in the morning. I've been up for a while. Long enough to brush my teeth, try to do something with my hair, borrow a shirt and make some breakfast. By the way, you need to get one of your lapdogs to go kidnap me a hairbrush. I'm going to assume that short nest on your head is the reason there's not even a comb in this place. Unless you want me to shave my head, I suggest finding me a few more necessities. For a guy that's been planning my 'seduction' for ages, you sure aren't very prepared to have a woman stay in your place."

Truth be told, she had been secretly glad there was zero evidence of women in his bachelor pad. Even though she planned on disappearing at the first opportunity, she hated to think of Tyson entertaining other women.

"Ouch, gorgeous!" he said. "Do you always wake up with such a sharp tongue?"

She shrugged. "I also had time to make and drink a pot of coffee. You sleep like the dead, Tyson King."

Tyson raised an eyebrow before answering. "Actually, I'm usually a restless sleeper. Your tight little pussy must have sapped all the strength right out of me."

Claudia blushed.

"And I wouldn't call Mercer a lapdog anywhere in his hearing. The guy can be touchy about the strangest things and he's not squeamish in saying so."

Tyson sat up and noticed a bowl and cup on his nightstand. "What's this? Did you cook for me?"

She nodded. "I brought you some breakfast and coffee. I was hoping we could talk once you woke up."

Tyson reached for the coffee. "That's amazing, babe. No one's ever done that for me before."

"Ummm... you might want to try it before praising me. I'm not known for my culinary prowess. There's a reason I eat at work most days and my pantry is a shoe closet. I didn't know what you took in your coffee so I put cream in it."

Tyson took a big gulp and clearly tried not to choke. It was cold, the cream slightly separated from the coffee. "Uh, when exactly did you make this?"

"About two hours ago. You slept for longer than I expected."

Tyson picked up the bowl and choked down a few bites of the soggy Rice Krispies before thanking her for her thoughtfulness and vowing to put locks on the fridge and pantry. "What did you want to talk about?" he asked, leaning back.

"What do you think?" She rolled her eyes and waved her arm around, indicating the room. "This."

His piercing eyes trapped her in place. "There's nothing to discuss. This is your new reality."

Claudia frowned darkly. "There are things to discuss, caveman. If you think keeping a woman is going to be all high heels and sexy times then you have another think coming."

"I do?" he drawled, clearly fighting a grin. "Please enlighten me, beautiful."

Claudia crossed her arms in front of her chest and gave him her best no nonsense look. She had been practicing what to say all morning. She just didn't know what his reaction might be to some of her demands.

"I left a list of my necessities downstairs on the island. Among them is the contents of my pantry," she held a hand up when he looked like he might speak, "which contrary to what you might think, I *cannot* live without. I also have very particular and expensive taste in clothes, and since you're a billionaire with a car elevator, I'm thinking you can accommodate me. The most necessary items are on the list. I'm also in the middle of a very important online game, so I expect my entire gaming setup to be brought over and installed. All of my bathroom products and, of course, Delaware."

"Delaware?" Tyson asked.

"My pet rock," she answered. "He's been my traveling companion since I started running and realized I couldn't exactly drag a pet around North America. Especially if I had to drop everything at a moment's notice."

Her breath hitched at the end, pain clouding her green eyes.

Tyson reached out and took her hand, pulling her closer. "No more running Claudia. I'll take care of things, you can count on that."

She nodded her head. She barely knew him, but if she were ever tempted to believe anyone it would be Tyson King. The man moved real estate all over the country with the wave of a hand. Dealing with men like Dante would be distasteful to the wealthy businessman, but for her, he would.

"That's why I wrote the second list," she said pulling a paper out from under the edge of a blanket.

"What's this?" Tyson asked gently, taking the list from her fingers and reading. "Yoga, guitar lessons, painting, shopping for art, pilates, girls' nights…" He raised an eyebrow.

"I haven't had a girls night out in years," she defended. "I bet a night out with Anya would be epic! And between you and that blond dude, my last girls night was ruined."

"Sitnikov? Over my dead body," Tyson growled. "That woman is deadly, and I mean that in every sense of the word. I forbid you from seeing her unaccompanied."

Claudia's face lit up. "But I can see her?"

Tyson chuckled, realizing how neatly she had maneuvered him. "You can do almost anything if it makes you happy. I even have a few additions for your list. I want you here with me, where I intend to keep you safe. But I don't want you to be unhappy."

Her face grew serious and she nodded slowly. "The only reason I'm agreeing to this twisted kidnapping is because I believe that." Her eyes traced over his muscular torso. "And because you're super hot and rock my bedroom world."

"Ah, shallow woman," he growled, reaching out to pull her down. He rolled them until she was crushed under his naked body. Her long hair tangled around them.

She gasped and pressed her hands against the massive chest hovering above her. Tyson nudged her legs apart with his thigh. She squirmed against him, moaning and thoroughly enjoying the feel of his hairy muscular leg rubbing against her intimately. Her hips jerked of their own volition when he stroked across her clit. She tilted her head back and panted in response.

"Are you sore, Claudia?" he asked, his voice a deep growl, muscles straining with need.

Claudia bit her lip, looked away from him and shook her head. He forced her to look at him with a hand on her jaw. "Truth, Claudia," he demanded.

She sighed in annoyance, "If I say yes, will you stop?"

He grinned, white teeth flashing against dark lips. "No baby, I'll just take a little more care. You're too fragile to risk."

She huffed a little. "Fine, yes, I'm sore."

She clutched him, her fingernails digging into his fore-arms, when he moved swiftly back and pulled her up with him. Stripping off the shirt she wore, he tossed her over his shoulder and stood with her. She squealed in surprise and braced her hands against his back. She stopped struggling when she realized she had an incredible and unique view of his rock hard ass flexing and releasing as he walked with her.

He entered the stone-tiled walk-in shower and turned on the taps. Claudia screamed as a burst of cold water hit her square in the ass right before it turned warm and then heated to a bearably hot temperature. Finally, Tyson lifted her by the waist and lowered her until she was standing in front of him with her back pressed against the wall. He took a bar of soap and started washing her, paying particular attention to the area between her legs.

Claudia was left gasping and mindless by the time his skillful fingers were finished soaping her. She no longer cared about any lingering soreness, wanting only to climb his body and lower herself onto his thick penis. If she had been physi-cally capable of attacking a man Tyson's size, she probably would have. "Please, Tyson," she begged him, "I want you so bad!"

He smiled and reached for the showerhead, pulling it down. His gaze captured hers with intense lust as he forced the head of the sprayer between her thighs and let the water hit her clitoris directly. Claudia gasped and flung her head back, resting it against the wall. She widened her stance for him and spread her arms out, hands splayed against the tiles. The water teased every part of her vagina, flicking her clit over and over again.

Pressure built up between her legs. She tilted her hips forward, mindlessly seeking the wonderful sensations he was forcing on her. Her breathing quickened, legs shook and eyes closed as she prepared to come. Just as her body began to convulse, he flicked something on the showerhead, driving the water pressure up harder against her. With a high-pitched scream, Claudia came hard, her legs folding underneath her.

Tyson dropped the showerhead and reached for her as she slid to the floor of the shower. With hands under her armpits he made sure she didn't hit the hard bottom painfully. Once her ass hit the floor of the shower he let her go. He tilted her chin up so her dreamy, clouded gaze met his. Standing over her, Tyson took his erect, throbbing cock into his hand and began stroking it. He was so incredibly turned on by Claudia's response that he looked as though he would take only a few moments to finish.

Understanding and lust flashed across her beautiful face. Claudia scrambled up to her knees underneath him and balanced herself against him with long, slender fingers against his thighs. Eyes never leaving hers, he groaned when she stuck her tongue out and tasted the head of his penis as it bobbed in his hand. He slapped it gently against her wicked mouth and revelled in the feeling of her tongue flick against the underside of him, tracing a path up to the slit.

"Fuck," he said between gritted teeth and reached out to put a fist against the wall. "I'm coming, baby."

She looked up at him eagerly, her blond hair darkened by the shower stream and clinging to her beautiful, curvy body.

He wanted nothing more than to come all over her, putting his mark on her in a barbaric display. She opened her mouth wide as semen shot from the end of his dark engorged cock. The first pump landed across her lips and tongue, the second and third hitting her gorgeous breasts.

He continued to stare down at her and nearly lost his mind when she reached up, smeared her finger through the fluid on her chest and brought it up to her lips. She was by far the sexist woman he had ever encountered. He reached down and pulled her to her feet, slamming his lips against hers in a possessive kiss. She returned the pressure of his lips with enthusiasm. After a few minutes of intense kisses, he finally set her on her feet and insisted they finish their shower.

CHAPTER EIGHT

I f Claudia's heart hadn't been ready to jump out of her chest with nerves, she would have smirked at the look of deadly bewilderment on Daniel's face. He was looking around the Victoria Secret shop like he expected there to be a pit of vipers around the next rack. Even funnier was the look on the salesgirl's face. She appeared awestruck by his handsome face and chiseled body, but clearly planned on keeping her distance from his constant expression of instant death to those that approach. This combination would work perfectly for Claudia's plan.

Claudia picked some items off the racks and asked to be shown to a change room. She quirked an eyebrow at Daniel and nodded her head toward the back. Like a good little bodyguard, he went to check the rooms. Only one of them was occupied and the middle-aged woman was clearly not an assassin. He backed off and waved Claudia in.

Claudia went into the room, dropped the armful of frothy items and waited patiently. She didn't remove the pair of jeans, blue long sleeved shirt or flat ballet shoes she wore. A few minutes later the shop girl came back to check on the two women. The other one was just finishing up.

"Actually, I do need a different size," Claudia said, handing over a black lacy nightgown. "I'll take this in a 14 and... can you please give these to my friend, Daniel. Ask him which of these he thinks will work for his boss."

The girl looked mortified at the idea of approaching the deadly man standing guard outside the change rooms like a feral dog. Claudia pressed several panty and bra sets into her hands and waved her off. Hopefully the super awkward conversation that was about to take place would keep both of them occupied for a few minutes while Claudia made a swift exit out the back door. She had noticed it before when shopping here, vigilant about her surroundings in case Dante was on her trail.

As she swiftly exited through the fire door she smiled, picturing Daniel looking down at the terrified girl with an expression of disinterest combined with murderous tendencies. She almost wished she could witness that. She only hoped he would take his time before becoming suspicious and deciding to check on her.

Once Claudia was in the alley and the door closed behind her, she ran full speed toward the other end and the entrance to the subway. Luckily for her, she knew the city like the back of her hand. She knew every possible escape route. She hoped for the best, but always anticipated the worst: that Dante, Franco and their thugs would discover her whereabouts. Now, thanks to Tyson King, that possibility was more likely than ever.

And yet, she couldn't bring herself to regret her brief time with the giant, possessive billionaire. She knew there was never going to be a happily ever after for her, but if anyone could make her dream it was Tyson. He had spent the past ten days doing his best to convince her that she should stay with him. His idea of convincing meant he kept her all but locked up in his tower of a penthouse, indulging in her every whim, including hiring instructors to teach her guitar lessons, painting, yoga and pilates. Claudia had quickly discovered she hated yoga and pilates and suspected she nearly got the instructor killed when she described some of the poses the man had made her do.

Claudia had giggled at the thunderous expression on Tyson's face around a mouthful of pasta that he'd made at her request. She had been in the process of explaining what a 'down dog' was, thoroughly enjoying the way his eyebrows lowered ominously over snapping eyes. The more time she spent with him the more possessive he became. Finally she had said with a gasping laugh, "I'm pretty sure my yoga teacher would be more interested in you than me."

Tyson had rounded the table, shoved her plate out of the way, bent her over the table and fucked her from behind in retaliation for her teasing. Then he had laid her naked in front of the fireplace in the living room and fed her the rest of her dinner by hand. No one did possessive sexy better than Tyson King.

Reflecting on the past week and half spent with her new boyfriend, Claudia realized she was going to miss the big, unpredictable man. Too bad she couldn't trust anyone. Dante taught her that lesson too well. The man had been all charm, good looks and easy money while wooing her. It wasn't until she was well and truly in his pocket that she realized his quick smile hid a vicious temper and that his charm and money were backed by drugs and prostitutes. She had understood, after enduring one of his more nasty drunken rants, that he intended to sell her to his friends for top dollar. She was his beautiful blond princess, relatively inexperienced except for him, she could help him get places by entertaining his competitors and gathering information.

Claudia was smart enough to make her escape the moment she discovered Dante's sadistic plans. She decided to take insurance with her in the form of a USB key with the contents of Dante's hard drive, in case her plan to lay low didn't work and she had to buy herself help. Though a suspicious guy, Dante never once thought Claudia would betray him. She was far too pliable and silent to give him any indication what she would run away from him – not when he could give her any pretty thing her heart desired, and buy prestige in their circle of Miami acquaintances. He hadn't known her true character one little bit. That's one thing she had to give Tyson credit for. He liked to buy her expensive things, but he never once acted like it made a difference to their relationship.

Ignoring the curious looks that followed her, Claudia pelted toward the subway stairs, virtually flying down them to the mid line. Barely pausing, she swiped her transit card before going through the turnstile. She landed on the platform, gasping for breath, and made her way behind a pillar to wait for a train. She didn't think there was any way Daniel was fast enough to get down here before a train came, but the guy was an eerie combination of intelligence and ruthless determination.

Claudia sighed in relief when a train pulled up. "Excuse me!" she said breathlessly, pushing past a group of midday shoppers. She ignored their grumbles and hopped on the train. Quickly finding a window seat she sat and stared toward the stairwell entrance, silently begging the train to get moving.

The train doors shut and within seconds the train was moving. She was in the process of slumping in her seat in relief when she saw Daniel leap down the stairs. Without pausing, he hurtled toward the nearest train door. As though instinctively knowing where to find her, his eyes zeroed in on her through the window and narrowed.

"No!" she gasped, shocked. She watched, terrified as he tried to force the doors open.

Damn him, Daniel had anticipated her. His usual stoic expression gave way to fury for a split second when he realized he wasn't able to pry the door of the moving train open. That look of fury convinced Claudia she never wanted to run into the ex-mercenary in a dark alley. She watched him with trepidation as the train gathered speed. He took his phone out of his pocket and lifted it to his ear. Then he pointed at her. Pinning her. She knew right down to her core he was marking her as prey for Tyson King.

Claudia forced her frozen brain to work over time. She quickly deduced that Tyson would soon have his people crawling all over every subway station in the city. She would have to abandon her original plan of taking the train to the bus station and buying a ticket out of the city and get off at the next stop. Hopefully she could make it far enough away from the station before Tyson was able to galvanize his security team. It didn't bear thinking what he might do with her once he got his hands on her.

With a start, Claudia realized she didn't doubt he would find her. Tyson had far more resources than she did. He would be watching the airport, the bus depot, the train station and every road out of the city. He would snatch her up and drag her back to his lair where she would be a sitting duck for Dante and Franco. Damn it, why couldn't he just let her go! Why did all the men in her life want to *own* her?

What am I doing? Claudia thought to herself, suddenly furious. *I'm no quitter. If I was, I'd be dead by now. I'll get the hell out of*

*this city and Tyson King can just kiss the backside of my ass on my
way out!*

Claudia stood as the subway train approached its next
platform. She walked toward the back of the train car. On her
way by a guy in his early twenties listening to loud music with
earbuds, she pretended to sway and fall sideways into his lap.
She blushed furiously and excused herself, leaning forward so
her long hair brushed his face. He brought hands up to steady
her and, after getting a good look at the bounty that literally
fell into his lap, his scowl turned into a grin. Claudia grinned
back and stood up, squeezing his shoulder. She continued
toward the nearest door with his black hoodie, which had
been carelessly tossed in the seat next to him, clutched in her
hand.

As soon as she was out the door, she pulled the Univer-
sity emblazoned sweater over her head and popped the
hood up, careful to tuck every last strand of hair into the
enveloping hood. Next she shoved the chic oversized
sunglasses on that she had lifted from a woman who was
too busy reading her text messages to notice the sticky
fingers that reached into her purse. Trusting that she
wouldn't draw undue notice to herself, Claudia made her
way back up to street level. This time she didn't run,
instead forcing herself to slouch and walk at a normal pace.
She had to blend into the street atmosphere – not a difficult thing as she was currently in a bustling part of
downtown.

Claudia knew her next move would draw Tyron right to
her, but she didn't have a choice. She would just have to trust
that lady luck would stick with her. She pulled out her cell
phone and called the only person she knew in the city who
might be capable of helping her out. Anastasia Sitnikov.

"Claudia!" Anya answered in a breathless rush. "Where
the hell have you been?"

Claudia laughed shortly. "Locked up in Tyson King's penthouse."

"Why didn't you call or text me?" Anya demanded, sounding miffed. "I was worried."

"Yeah, same goes, girl. Last I saw of your ass it was being dragged out of that awful gambling club by super hot blond guy." Claudia snorted. "Look, Anya, I don't have a lot of time here, so I'm going to explain some things to you fast. I'm living here illegally, I don't have a work Visa or anything and I'm Canadian."

Anya said nothing for a moment and then said sarcastically, "Are you some kind of Canadian terrorist then? Did you steal the maple syrup recipe and decide to sell it on the black market to your neighbours to the south."

Claudia rolled her eyes. "I'm serious Anya. I moved here a few years ago to dance in Vegas. I met a guy there, the owner of the casino where I danced. He introduced me to a colleague, a guy from Miami. I thought I was in love, but it all turned out really badly. He was some kind of big time drug dealer, into all kinds of terrible things. He... he tried to make me do things. I knew refusing would end badly for me so I grabbed something of his and took off. Now he, and god knows who else, are probably after me. I need to get out of the city fast and I don't know anyone else that might be able to help." She finished in a breathless rush, waiting anxiously for Anya's reply.

Anya seemed to digest what she said for a moment before speaking slowly, "So you were a Vegas showgirl? How did I not know this about you? That explains so much."

Claudia laughed out loud, slapping a hand over her mouth so she wouldn't draw attention to herself. "I sucked as a showgirl, but somehow I caught Dante's attention. Lucky me."

"I might be speaking totally out of my ass here," Anya said, "but I was under the impression Tyson King had a thing for you. He's a powerful guy, he can probably keep you safer than anyone else in the city, except maybe my brother."

Claudia sighed heavily. "You don't understand, Anya. I just can't be under the thumb of another guy, especially one who's not up front about his business. I let myself be led by my ex-boyfriend, and it ended so badly I had to change my name and stop speaking to my family." Her voice broke on the last word. "I don't trust anyone to take care of me but me."

"I understand better than you think darling, one day I'll tell you all about it," Anya said quietly. "In the meantime, let me think for a second."

Claudia held her breath while she waited, chewing on the ragged edge of a fingernail. She wanted to tell Anya to hurry, that Tyson would most likely be tracing her phone as they spoke. Her gaze darted around the sidewalk and street. She saw a few guys on the other side wearing suit jackets over jeans. They were thickly muscled and wearing dark sunglasses. She didn't know them personally, but she did recognize the walk and the sweeping glances they took. They were some kind of security. Claudia darted into a nearby Chinese tea shop and watched them through the window until they rounded the end of the block.

"Claudia?" Anya's voice sounded worried as though she had tried to get the other girl's attention a few times.

"Yes, I'm here," she replied quickly. "Sorry, I thought I saw someone that could belong to Tyson."

"Okay, here's what you're going to do," Anya said, all business now that she recognized the real fear in her friend's voice. "You're going to go see my brother. I'll call him and tell him to expect you. He'll be happy to do me a solid. Especially if I promise him an extra month of living in his mansion, enjoying full time live-in staff and an Olympic-sized swimming pool."

Claudia grinned despite herself. Anya really was a gem. "Maybe I could move in too?"

Anya laughed and gave her the address. Without hanging up, Claudia dropped her phone into the shop's wastebasket. Tyson could enjoy tracking it while she was on her way to the other side of the city. Taking a deep breath and pulling the hood further over her face, Claudia walked swiftly out of the shop and hailed the first cab she saw.

CHAPTER NINE

Claudia gaped at the man that opened the door of Vladimir Sitnikov's mansion. He was probably even bigger than Tyson, which was saying something considering Tyson was one of the largest men to inhabit her world. This guy was probably close to seven feet, dwarfing her own not insubstantial frame. His hair was cut close to his skull, which highlighted the stark tattoos that wound up his neck into his hairline. He wore a dress shirt with a leather holster over top. Tucked under both of his arms were lethal looking guns. His bearded jaw looked perpetually tensed in steely determination. Her eyes remained glued on his massive hands, watching for any twitch that might indicate he was reaching for a weapon. Dude looked like he should be carrying an axe.

She wondered if his name was Tiny.

"Are you the butler?" she asked weakly, eyeing him skeptically. She was pretty certain the Sitnikov mansion would be on everyone's no-solicitation list if this dude was answering the door regularly. She was intensely glad she wasn't a Jehovah's Witness at that moment.

"Claudia?" He asked in a heavily accented voice. Her name sounded like *Clow-dee-yah* coming out of his mouth.

She nodded, but briefly considered saying no and running away. She could probably scale the massive privacy gate that had swung open to let her in if she was properly motivated – like being shot at by a Russian mobster for trespassing. She wondered how Anya was brave enough to live here with this human pit bull around.

"Boss will see you."

He moved back to let her in. Knowing her options were slim to none Claudia took a breath and entered into the darkened interior of the house that belonged to the most feared man in the city. Even in her relatively small and sheltered circle at the coffee shop she worked at, she heard his name mentioned in whispers. Usually in connection to some illicit business or mob activity. She hadn't realized until several days ago that her friend was his sister. But she trusted Anya. With her life, apparently.

The mountain of a man strode down a hall in front of her. Claudia would have enjoyed looking around her at the beautiful furnishings of the mansion, but his legs ate up the hall, leaving her to nearly run to keep up. He stopped abruptly next an ornate, carved wooden door. He banged on it twice with a fist before shoving it open.

Claudia hesitated. He reached a hand out for her and ushered her impatiently into the room with a massive paw against her back. She gasped as she was propelled forward into a gorgeous masculine office. The door slammed shut at her back, trapping her in with one of the scariest men she would ever meet – and that includes Franco Delgado.

Vladimir Sitnikov stood behind his desk. She eyed him as covertly as she could, feeling completely overwhelmed in the mansion and in his presence. She silently questioned his relation to the spunky, smart-mouthed Anya. His sister was lovely and lithe, like a tiny dancer figurine. While Vladimir was much taller, leanly muscled and surrounded with a menacing intensity that stole her breathe and had her questioning her sanity in deliberately seeking him out.

Claudia watched him warily, ready to fly at the first hint of Russian mob-ittude. Not that she had a hope in hell of getting past the human-shaped guard dog that stalked the premises. Vladimir stopped in front of her, looking down into her face intently. He was close enough that she could see grey in his dark hair and lines of strain fanning out from his eyes and lips. He looked implacable, as though his iron hold on a huge empire was unshakable. It took its toll though, and made him seem somehow lonely. Which made him slightly more human in her eyes.

He brought a hand up to her face. His fingers were long and rough. The middle one had an ornate ring on it that she suspected was Russian. The finger was crooked as though it had been badly broken once. She flinched, but forced herself to hold still when he pushed the hood back off her head. Without asking permission, he took a hand full of her hair and pulled it out from the hoodie, running his fingers down the long, wavy length. It flowed like a silk banner over her generous breasts down to her waist.

"Beautiful," he murmured, dropping the lock of hair and stepping away from her. "I see how you have managed to capture the kingpin's attention. You would be a rare prize for the man."

Claudia frowned. She was getting sick of men thinking they could touch her without permission. She tucked the silken strand of hair behind her ear and stared up at Vladimir. He was studying her intently. She didn't like the way he spoke of Tyson, like a business acquaintance or something. Finally she found her voice and said, "Anya said you could help me, Mr. Sitnikov."

Her words seemed to snap his focus away from his musings. "Please, call me Vladimir my dear. I apologize for my poor manners. It is just that I have long wondered if anything could crack the money machine that is Tyson King. It's interesting to me that a young woman like yourself is the one to finally break into his exclusive tower."

Claudia snorted. "I don't remember it happening quite that way."

He stared at her with chilling intensity. She really got the feeling that he was weighing how valuable she could be if used against the billionaire tycoon. She shivered at the thought of these two men clashing and really, really hoped that, for her sake, Anya hadn't sent her into the lion's den to be consumed. She knew there would be no way off his property without his express permission. Despite its outward charming exterior, she suspected she was currently standing in the middle of a modern day fortress.

Crossing her arms in front of her chest she glared at him. "Anya would be extremely pissed if anything happened to me because of you."

He laughed, the sound deep and slightly unused. As though very little amused him enough to warrant laughter. She felt privileged. And also a lot like a little mouse trying to convince a lion not to eat her.

"Yes, she would be annoyed," he replied still eyeing her. "I can see why she has befriended you, Miss Cantore. You both possess a fighting spirit. This is something I can admire in a woman. Even if the fight is useless."

"What's that supposed to mean?" she asked defiantly.

Vladimir went around behind his desk and sat in the big, dark chair. It looked like an extension of his body, comfortable, like a place from which he spent a lot of time running his vast empire. "What I mean, Claudia Cantore, is that you should go back to Tyson King and beg his forgiveness. Then ask him prettily to take care of this messy business you have found yourself in."

Claudia's temper soared. She assumed Anya must have told her brother a few details. And no doubt he had enough contacts to fill in the rest if he chose to be informed on her background. Given her involvement with his beloved sister, Claudia had to assume he would have done some checking up on her before she arrived on his doorstep.

"I don't need any man to take care of me!" she snapped. "The last time I let a guy treat me like a pretty little doll he beat me up and tried to prostitute me out to his buddies. If you aren't going to help me get out of this city, then you can get out of my way. Let me the hell out of this place and I'll do it on my own. I've run before without help, I can do it again."

Vladimir's eyebrows lowered and his dark eyes glowed with an unholy light that had Claudia clutching herself and stepping back. What had she been thinking, mouthing off to such a lethal man? A long, jagged scar that bisected his jaw twitched in barely suppressed fury. *Well this is it Claudia*, she thought with a sigh, *you're about to pay the piper for continually stumbling into the path of terrifying mobster guys.*

"I didn't know this," he said quietly and almost... *soothingly?* He continued, "I would not wish that experience on any woman. Of course, it would be my privilege to help you in your moment of need."

Claudia felt her jaw drop, but she was powerless not to gape. Something about what Dante had tried to do to her got under this guy's powerful skin. Anya had told her that she could sympathize. Suddenly Claudia felt sick. What had happened to Anya that she could understand Claudia's situation? What had happened to make her brother more willing to help a woman in distress?

For the first time Claudia pondered the idea of staying and confronting Dante and Franco. With men like Tyson

King and Vladimir Sitnikov at her back, and a friend like Anya at her side, she might actually survive. But as soon as the thought occurred to her it flitted out of her brain. She just couldn't bring herself to trust another man that wanted to lock her up and take care of her, as much as her body craved the possessive touch of her new lover.

Vladimir's calculating eyes followed her every micro-expression. She was glad she didn't have to do business with the chilling intense man. She could only imagine the people in his orbit pinned on the other side of that gaze, wondering if he was determining their use to him and whether they were better to him alive or dead. She shivered.

His sharp eyes took note. "I will have Boris show you to a room where you can rest for a few moments while I make arrangements for your journey."

Relief flooded through her, making Claudia feel light headed. She knew Vladimir Sitnikov was as good as his word. A man in his position would have to be. She wanted to smile and thank him. Tell him that she was grateful.

Instead, in typical Claudia fashion, she said, "Seriously!? Your butler's name is actually Boris?"

CHAPTER TEN

Tyson King hit disconnect on his cell phone and dropped it onto his desk. He leaned back in his huge chair, ignoring the ominous creak. It'd taken several hours longer than he'd expected, but he finally had a location on the girl. His hands and his dick both pulsed with need. He wanted to strangle her, caress her, chain her to him and fuck her until she couldn't think of doing anything so stupid again.

The unfamiliar terror he had felt when Mercer had called earlier to say he was looking at her as she rapidly disappeared by herself on a city train was nearly overwhelming. Claudia couldn't handle herself. She was too soft. If her ex got his hands on her, or even worse, the scum that was Franco Delgado, they would snap her neck without hesitating. She wasn't safe. And the woman wasn't doing herself any favours by running the first chance she got. She was too easy to track.

Now, her safety was confirmed and his fear for her life morphed rapidly into all consuming fury. How *dare* she put herself in danger? His fist crashed down on the desk in front of him causing everything to jump. His water glass rolled onto its side, splashing water across some acquisition papers.

He ignored the damage and stood. Rolling his massive shoulders in his suit jacket, he swiftly turned to the window of his office tower, which overlooked the downtown business district.

Popping his knuckles, he picked his phone back up and called Mercer. His loyal man answered the phone on the first ring. "I know where she is."

"Is she safe?" Mercer asked swiftly.

Any tension Tyson might have felt toward his bodyguard's loss of Claudia dissipated. Mercer didn't show emotions. Ever. Yet he unbent enough to inquire after Claudia's well-being, which indicated he felt some regard for her. Even if it was just as the boss' woman. Claudia was a clever woman. If she had been determined to run, she would've bided her time until the opportunity arose. It was probably only a matter of time before one of them lost her, despite their years of iron control and vigilance. As testified by her ability to stay alive since fleeing Miami, Claudia had a well-honed sense of survival.

"She's safe. For now," Tyson said. "I want you and two of your guys to accompany me to her location. Bring bags. We'll be staying for a few days. I need some time with Claudia, to show her why this behaviour is unacceptable. I don't want her back in the city until I can trust her."

"Done," Mercer replied. "I can get Theo and Brandon. She's met both of them."

"Have a car around to pick me up in the next five minutes. We leave the city as soon as you and your men are ready."

"I'll have them ready in fifteen."

"Good." Tyson hung up. He loosened his tie and dropped his phone into his pocket.

He looked back out over the city, wondering if one of the moving lights far below his tower was his Claudia speeding away from him in the fading light of the evening. He breathed in deeply, attempting to control some of the anger he felt. He would have to teach her why she must never run from him. But he was a big man and he could too easily hurt the delicate woman if he lost his temper with her. He would have to control some of the rage and lust coursing through his veins, demanding him to find his woman and chain her to him irrevocably. Lucky for her, he had a three hour drive ahead of him to contemplate how not to break her while disciplining her.

The remote cabin hadn't been easy to find, but Vladimir's detailed directions, written out in scrawling cursive, led her to the right place on the first try. She had nearly missed the turn off for the road in the heavily forested area, but had seen it in the sweep of her headlights at the last moment. She'd slowed her borrowed car down and pulled it onto the dirt track. She winced a little as the gorgeous black Mercedes bumped along the winding, hole filled drive.

She knew she was in the right place when she drove up to the entrance. It was exactly as Vladimir had described. The lovely cabin looked deceptively small and rustic from the outside. He had assured her it would have all the amenities she would need to last for years if she chose to stay and hide out. Claudia hoped she could somehow resolve things before that long. She was a city girl at heart. Not that she didn't love the cabin on first sight, but she wasn't in to roughing it. Bears and ticks were on her list of things that she'd like never to experience up close and personal. Right below Dante and Franco.

With no luggage she made her way easily up to the front door and entered the code that Vladimir had given her. The door unlocked and she pushed it open. She realized immediately just how deceptive the 'cabin' was when she wandered in, her mouth opening in delight and awe. It vaguely reminded her of Tyson's penthouse with its wealthy rustic charm. The main floor boasted wall to ceiling windows that she was sure in daylight would showcase a stunning view of the mountains.

She counted two bedrooms and an office on the main floor as well as a sprawling kitchen with everything she would need. A walk-in pantry proved to her exactly how stocked up she would be. She could survive on many of the items without ever having to figure out the complex looking stove. She decided against exploring the dark basement until daylight. Her tired, overactive imagination was more than likely going to see an axe murderer (or Boris) in every shadow.

Wandering into the living room she looked up and whispered 'wow' as she took in the loft that soared high above her head at the top of a wooden staircase. She grinned and trailed her fingers across the smooth wooden railing as she headed up. She wished, when she reached the top, that it was daylight and she could see out across the lake valley.

Instead, she would have to make do with the huge low platform bed that filled the space and all the other luxurious amenities she would be forced to enjoy. A gorgeous painting of what she assumed must be the lake surrounded by autumn trees rested over a fireplace across the room from the bed. In front of the fireplace was a single, huge leather chair that looked well loved and well used.

On further inspection of the top floor, she discovered a massive tub that could double as a pool. "He did tell me to make myself comfortable..." she murmured her hands going to the zipper of her borrowed jacket.

She felt like Goldilocks, discovering a warm, welcoming abode that would fit her quite well after all of her trials.

Letting the jacket fall to the floor she leaned over the lip of
the huge tub, plugged in the stopper and turned on the water.
She trailed her fingers through the pressurized stream and
made adjustments until the heat of the water was just right.
With a sigh, she stood and began stripping her clothes.

She studied herself in the mirror over the sink as she let
each garment fall to her feet. She looked like the same volup-
tuous blond that had tried and failed to become a showgirl on
the Vegas strip. Her big breasts and hips had slowed her
down compared to the other girls. But her perfectly shaped
lips, prominent cheekbones and innocent green eyes had
bought her place on the stage. With a small smile, she struck
a showgirl pose. One leg up and bent as though propped up
by a four-inch heel. The other leg was long and straight. She
threw one arm up over her head in presentation, tilted her
head back and curved her spine to thrust her breasts out.

Claudia crossed her eyes and stuck her tongue out at the
image. She gathered her long, wavy hair on top of her head
and tied it with one of the many hair ties she used as acces-
sories so she would always have one available. She slid into
the tub with a deep sigh and relaxed completely into the
warm embrace as her bare bottom came to rest on a bench.
She tilted her head back and sank down until her shoulders
and most of her neck was under the water. Tendrils of hair,
escapees from her hastily tied up hair, floated in the water
around her. She idly trailed fingers across the top of the tub
until her exploration yielded a button, which she pushed to
turn on the jets, filling the tub with bubbles.

Claudia enjoyed the energetic jets as they danced around
her body. She relaxed completely and stared out of the single
window in the room into the darkness of her new mountain
home. She was definitely liking it here more and more with
every passing moment. Lazily, she reached for the soap and
began running it over her wet body. Each stroke felt like the

hands of her lover caressing her abundant curves. Images of the erotic shower she had shared with Tyson several days ago flooded her mind. Claudia hastily put the soap down. She turned around and kneeled on the bench propping her arms up on the edge of the tub. With a sigh, she lazily stared into the darkness and thought of the generosity of her benefactor.

She was deeply impressed with Vladimir Sitnikov's good taste. She wouldn't have expected it of a man that surrounded himself with heavy, masculine furniture that looked old world Russian. In fact, she had even more trouble picturing him out here in the wilderness than her city-raised self. She had no problem picturing Tyson King's big body resting sprawled out in the massive tub. Or on the huge bed. And in one of the big leather chairs next to the fireplace. And working in the kitchen, with all of its modern amenities.

With a gasp Claudia sat up, water pouring over her shoulders and down her back. "No!" she said out loud, eyes wide and staring into the darkness beyond the door. "He wouldn't..."

But why would Vladimir Sitnikov set her up? He had seemed so sincere in his wish to help her. Maybe she was being paranoid. Claudia stood up and, ignoring the streaming water, swiftly exited the tub. She snatched a towel from the rack and dabbed at her body as she headed for the bedroom closet, heedless of the watery footprints she left on the hardwood floor.

She flung open the closet, snapped on the light switch and stepped inside. Though most of the clothes in the closet were more suited to wilderness – jeans, T-shirts, sweaters – she saw that there were a few business suits with dress shirts. She reached for one of the dress shirts and, dropping her towel, pulled it on. She ignored the way it clung to her wet body and buttoned it up. With dawning realization she knew, without a doubt, that she was wearing a shirt that belonged to Tyson

King. It swam on her, falling down to her knees, the sleeves reaching past her hands.

"Son of a BITCH!"

Whirling around, Claudia ran. She grabbed her purse and car keys, where she had dropped them on the bed and ran down the flight of stairs. She didn't bother to dress in something more appropriate. She could figure it out along the way. If Vladimir Sitnikov sent her to Tyson King's cabin deep in the woods, the big dark-skinned devil wouldn't be far behind. And he would be pissed.

She flung the front door open to find the man himself standing on his own porch, waiting for her. His eyes glinted down at her with a mixture of triumph and something much darker. He was furiously angry with her. Claudia stumbled back a step, clutching tightly to her purse.

"Stop, Claudia," his deep voice growled. He stepped over the threshold and reached for her.

CHAPTER ELEVEN

Claudia threw her purse at him and whirled around, sprinting for the back door. Luckily, her perpetually on-edge brain had taken note of its whereabouts. She heard Tyson running behind her and tried for more speed. Her bare feet easily gripped the floor as she rounded the kitchen and reached for the door. She turned the lock, losing precious seconds, and flung it open. She hurtled into the darkness, heedless of the fact that she was unlikely to get far even if she managed to make it to the car barefoot.

"Oomph!" The air rushed out of her as she ran headlong into the rock solid body of Daniel Mercer. The guy she had vowed never to run into in the dark. So far she was doing a terrible job of taking care of herself.

Daniel didn't even flinch when she hit him full tilt. He simply absorbed her weight, his arms coming down around her, trapping her against his hard body. She squeaked in fear and tried to extricate herself from his punishing grip. He seemed quite determined to hang onto her until his boss arrived, which was a few seconds later. She realized from his terrifying strength that Daniel could snap her in two with little effort. He easily handed her off to Tyson and then melted into the darkness without a word.

Tyson re-entered the house, holding her easily in an iron grip. He shut the door and locked it behind him. Claudia found it disconcerting that Daniel wasn't coming in the house. She felt certain he, and maybe others, would guard them in the darkness. But whatever Tyson King had planned for her would take place in the privacy of the house. They might be able to hear her screams, but she knew without a doubt that not a single one of them would interfere. She was once more under the control of a very powerful man. And he wasn't happy with her.

She tried pulling her arm from his grip, but he held her tightly, dragging her along with him as he secured the front door and hefted a bag up over his broad shoulder. Claudia shivered as the cool air caressed her damp body. "Let me go," she demanded, pulling her arm harder.

Tyson ignored her completely and pulled her along as he turned lights out on his way to the staircase. He dragged her up the stairs and into the bedroom. He finally let her go, pushing her toward the bed. "Stay," he snapped when she hit the edge and tumbled onto the mattress.

Claudia righted herself and sat up straight, watching warily as he dropped his bag on the floor, turned his back on her and knelt in front of the fireplace, opening the flue and swiftly working to set up kindling and newspaper. Claudia stood, hugging herself uncertainly and looking toward the stairs. She could probably make it at least partway – maybe all the way – before he caught up with her.

"Don't," his voice rumbled. "Mercer isn't happy with you right now. I wouldn't recommend giving him a reason to put his hands on you again. He may be my man, but he's also a viciously effective militant that doesn't distinguish between the sexes when he decides to take down an enemy."

Claudia shivered in apprehension and let her legs collapse underneath her until she was perched on the edge of the bed. She decided it would be best to give Daniel some time to forget how she took off on his watch. Even though she sensed an implacable element in Tyson's movements that didn't bode well for her future comfort, she knew he was far less likely to do her irreparable harm than his terrifying bodyguard.

"Where did you find him?" she asked curiously, trying to break the heavy silence of the room with conversation.

Tyson didn't say anything for a minute and she thought he wasn't going to answer her idle question. When he spoke his voice was low and thoughtful. "His team was recommended to me when I had business in the DPRK. Something came up while we were trying to get back out of the country. Most of Mercer's guys were killed, cut down in front of us, but he worked like a machine. Taking the attackers on one at a time. He was shot twice. It still took awhile for him to go down, but eventually he weakened. I was able to finish them off and pull him out. He's stuck by my side ever since. I think he would stay even if I refused to pay him."

Claudia wasn't sure why he decided to tell her the truth of their grim story, but somehow it softened her toward them. They had overcome bad odds and made it out alive, forging a bond. Mercer would watch the back of the man he saved, and who had in turn saved him, like a loyal dog ready to rip out the throat of anyone that threatened the giant man. Together they maintained Tyson's empire. One built it while the other protected it.

Tyson struck a match and lit the paper, sitting back on his haunches and watching as the kindling caught fire. After a moment, he gently added a log to the fledgling fire, then pushed himself to his feet. He turned and looked at Claudia where she sat on the bed, her body enveloped in one of his shirts, her long bare legs bent in front of her.

"Come here, Claudia."

Her breath caught in her throat and she shook her head leaning back, away from the intense heat of his gaze. He took a few steps toward her and reached out to flick off the light. Now they were bathed in the soft glow of the fire. She shivered in the cool air of the mountain night, apprehension pinging through her.

"I said, come here, Claudia." Even though she couldn't see his face clearly in the dim lighting there was no mistaking the hard edge to his voice. He had something planned for her.

"What are you going to do?" she whispered into the darkness.

Impatient, he reached for her and hauled her to her feet. She tried slapping at his hands, but her efforts were useless. "Tyson!" she cried out when he reached for the shirt and easily lifted it over her head, bringing her arms up forcefully, and flinging the shirt into a corner. She shivered, naked in front of him, worried, but also defiant. She had no idea what he intended to do to her, but if he wanted her naked she could probably guess at least some of what he wanted.

"Please, Tyson," she asked as he reached for his bag. "Let's talk. I'm sorry you're upset, but I had to leave. You as much as said you led Dante and Franco right to me. I had to get out of there before they found a way to get to me."

She realized right away she had said the wrong thing when she felt his huge body stiffen in anger. His hand tightened, flexing his taut arm and causing his tattoos to ripple ominously. She felt vulnerable, standing naked at his mercy before him. He opened the zip on the bag, pulled something out then dropped the bag back on the floor. She gasped when he reached up and gripped her by the neck. He pulled her up against his chest, forcing her up on her tiptoes, and taking her lips in a ferocious kiss. His massive fingers flexed against her throat, not hurting, but showing her the strength he was capable of. She was like a butterfly fluttering uselessly against his superior musculature.

He pulled back a scant inch. Her fingers flew to her neck, landing on the steely grip of his fingers. When he spoke, his warm, spicy breath caressed her lips. "I don't want to hear you speak his name again."

Confused, her mind a muddled haze of fear and the beginnings of lust, she asked, "Who?"

"You don't get to speak Dante Marquez's name again. He's out of your life for good. Do you understand?" His intensity surprised and confused her.

"Not really," she breathed, her head swimming with the delicious scent of him. What was wrong with her? The guy was close to wringing her neck and yet her body was begging her to close the distance between them.

Tyson growled and shook her a little, his hold on her neck tightening fractionally. "You belong to me now. After this stunt, I'm not willing to allow you an inch of the patience I was willing to give you at the penthouse. You *will* learn what it means to be my woman, Claudia. I don't want to hear the name of your ex-lover pass those lips. Do you understand me now?"

Her lips parted in surprise. She'd seen the edge of a barbarian in some of his behaviour when he took her out of the club and chased her through his garage, but she thought that was the worst. She had no idea this savage, possessive side to him existed. She wasn't sure if she should be flattered or terribly worried.

"I understand," she whispered, stroking her hand soothingly over his wrist and down his flexed forearm. "Please, Tyson, what are you going to do to me?"

His grip on her neck loosened and his hand trailed down the front of her body, pausing briefly over the hardened peaks of her full breasts and brushing gently across the well-maintained strip of blond pubic hair. He brought his other hand up and snapped something on her wrist. The fingers of her other hand flew to her wrist to inspect the object. It was some kind of wide leather cuff with several short chain links, a few inches long in total, hanging from it. She frowned and felt around for the latch, but her agile fingers quickly discovered that it would not open to her. He had locked it.

"Tyson!" she snapped. "Stop it! I'm not playing kinky games with you right now. Get it off me."

His huge hand covered the bare wrist of her other hand and in seconds she was securely padlocked into the leather cuffs, short chains trailing down from each. She tugged and pulled at the cuffs, but they didn't budge. She stared angrily up at the big man. "What exactly do you think you're doing?" she demanded.

"I'm teaching my woman how to relinquish control and trust someone to take care of her."

Claudia's temper soared and she snarled, "Fuck that! Take this shit off of me right this instant, Tyson King! I'm not your plaything."

She felt his temper spark to match hers. She gasped apprehensively and stumbled back in escape. Her legs hit the bed and without her arms to balance her she would have fallen if he hadn't caught her. He gripped both of her wrists tightly over the leather padding. She whimpered as her body weight was dragged upward by her arms.

"You'll learn, Claudia," he snarled, his full lips pulled back, black against the white of his teeth. He looked so implacable in that moment she cried out in fear as he released her to tumble back on the bed.

"Tyson, let's talk about this," Claudia gasped as she bounced on the bed, some of her temper diffusing as she began to get worried. "I'm not really into bondage."

He ignored her and bent down to dig through the bag

some more. The muscles of his arms strained against the fabric of his white dress shirt. She couldn't see what he was pulling out of the bag, but the rustling made her anxious. She tried to reason with him again, this time going for firm rather than pleading. "Don't you dare put anything else on me Tyson King, or I will make you regret it. Your other girlfriends might be into this kinky shit, but I'm having nothing to do with it."

"I bought this stuff for you, before we even met. Never used it before," he rumbled in reply, straightening.

Claudia's head swam with the idea that he was planning on using this stuff on her before he even acquired her. She was pretty sure that was stalkerrific, but her pussy tingled at the thought that he always planned on tying her down for his use. Maybe she was as sick as he was. Damn her body for always responding so readily to him.

Firelight caressed the leather cuffs and some kind of rope held in his giant fist. He bent over and captured one of her ankles. Claudia gave a token effort to pull her ankle back but he held her fast. She heard the click as the leather cuff locked over the delicate bones of her ankle. The slither of sturdy rope over her calf caused her to shiver. He moved it off her skin with a brush of his fingers and proceeded to trap her other ankle.

She didn't understand right away what all of the rope and cuffs were about. At first she thought he was going to go with a standard spread eagle position (standard for other BDSM couples, *not* standard for her), but the short chains indicated otherwise. Claudia let out a panicked squeal when he grabbed her by the waist and flipped her over onto her stomach. She immediately tried to roll onto her back, but he brought a heavy hand down on her ass in a single warning spank.

"Stay put woman," he growled at her, the emphasis he put

on each word telling her he was still pretty pissed off at her for running.

Claudia forced herself to lay still as he maneuvered her limbs. Part of her was curious about what he intended to do. He clearly wanted to render her helpless, punish her for running away from him and disobeying his stupid rules. He arranged her on the bed with her arms and legs straight until he bent her leg at the knee and brought her heel up to her butt. He picked up her wrist and pulled on the short chain until her wrist almost reached her ankle. She heard a snap and rolled her head to the side to see what he was doing. Messy hair falling from the topknot she had arranged for her bath flopped in her eyes.

Claudia instinctively tried to pull her wrist back, but her ankle came with it. The same thing happened when she tugged on her ankle, her wrist pulled. She was completely stuck with her arm and leg raised over her ass. She frowned as he went around to the other side and latched her wrist to her ankle again. She felt as though she were being hogtied except her right limbs weren't attached to her left limbs. When he stepped away from the bed she decided to test the strength of her bonds. If she could somehow wiggle out of them she'd hit the ground running as fast as she could and then lock herself in the bathroom.

She peeked over at Tyson. He was kneeling next to the bed with the rope. Claudia tried rolling onto her side, grunting as her arms and legs protested. She gasped and quickly rolled back onto her belly. Tyson ignored her struggles as he rounded the other side of the bed and did something with the rope over there too. He kneeled on the bed next to her and pulling the rope up, latched it to a metal loop on the ankle restraint.

"Tyson, what are you doing to me?" Claudia's voice rose as she realized exactly how helpless she was about to become.

He held her still with a hand on her ankle, stretched his long arm out to the other side of the bed and pulled on the rope on the other side. Claudia gasped in surprise as the ankle and wrist already attached to the rope pulled outward, opening her up in a doggy-style sort of deal. Tyson snapped the latch shut on the other side, connecting the rope. Both of her knees were forced out, opening her pussy from behind. She tried wriggling, but realized quickly that the rope was looped under the bed and pulled taut so there was zero slack.

Tyson stepped back from the bed, inspecting his handiwork. Claudia visualized herself from that angle and blushed furiously. Her ankles were raised up over her thighs and spread to the sides giving him an unimpeded view of her pussy and ass. Her wrists, which were attached by the short chains to her ankles, were several inches below her feet and a few inches above the bed. The position should have been extremely uncomfortable, but the roping was arranged so there wasn't much pressure on her wrists or ankles.

Claudia was completely helpless. She had never been tied down like this before and wasn't sure she enjoyed it much. Though she had to admit that the thought of Tyson seeing her like this and enjoying the view heated her up in unexpected ways. Claudia licked her suddenly dry lips and said, "Can we please talk about this Tyson?"

He stepped up to the bed. She could see something dark and silky dangling from his fingers. "We had plenty of time to talk about your comfort zone at the penthouse. Now I think its time to make you understand a few things about me, Claudia."

He kneeled on the bed between her spread legs. She moaned when he bent over her back, the body heat from his huge body engulfing her, his thigh brushing erotically against her spread pussy. She wondered, as his leg stroked against her, sending a jet of pleasure through her, if she would leave evidence of her arousal on his expensive trousers. He leaned across her, his broad chest pressed to her back, his lips next to her ear.

"I've built an empire," he murmured, "out of controlling everyone and everything around me. I was willing to give you the opportunity to walk with me at my side, but you ran from me Claudia."

She shivered helplessly as he slipped a black silk blindfold over her eyes, cutting off her vision and taking away yet another element of her control. "Tyson..." she whispered. "I had to go, I'm sorry."

His shoulders hovered above her back, engulfing her slimmer torso. "I'm not sorry," he said.

"But... I thought you were mad?" she said breathlessly.

"Yes," he replied, planting his fists in the bed next to her body and levering himself up. "I'm extremely angry that you put yourself in danger. If Marquez or Delgado got hold of you, you wouldn't last ten minutes. I'm also annoyed that you went to the most powerful mobster in our city for help *over me.*"

Claudia sensed his anger as though it were a living thing and flinched. She hadn't really thought of it that way. She had been running away from the idea of being in a powerful man's control again and the potential that her enemies could find her. She didn't realize he might take offence that she would run to a business rival.

"No, Claudia, I'm not sorry," he continued. "Because you've given me exactly what I wanted. I tried it your way. I tried wooing you. Now I intend to chain you to my side."

Claudia's chest swelled with mixed emotions. She was annoyed that he could treat her so barbarically, that he *wanted* to treat her that way. She could also argue with his idea of 'wooing' her, considering he'd snatched her from an underground casino and forced her to live in his penthouse for more than a week. But a part of her acknowledged that, even furious, he wasn't hurting her. *Yet.* She really didn't mind the idea of being tied to him either, figuratively or literally. He was by far the sexist man she had ever encountered and he seemed happy to lavish her with whatever her heart desired. Except the opportunity to run away and possibly get herself killed.

"What are you going to do to me Tyson?" she asked, forcing herself to relax into the bonds so her muscles wouldn't get sore.

He lifted himself off of her, trailing a hand down her back and across her buttocks. She shivered at the contact and wiggled a little, seeking the warmth of his hand as he lifted it off her. "I intend to make you wait, Claudia. You can feel as helpless as I felt when I found out you were missing. You can feel the agony of time spent wondering where I'm at and if I'll come to you."

"I don't understand."

He ignored her and reached for something else. She heard more rustling and then he said, "But first..."

Claudia shrieked as something cold and gooey hit her square on the anus. She continued to gasp and struggle against her binding as he spread what she assumed was lubricant against her asshole. She had never been touched there, let alone penetrated. She pressed her hips in the bed as much as she could, but the movement forced her arms back uncomfortably. He began to wiggle a finger into the tight hole. "Tyson!" she gasped. "We need to talk about this!"

He paused, giving her time to adjust. His deep voice rumbled over her. "Are you denying me Claudia? Is that really what you want?" His hot breath caressed her ass cheek as he bit into the flesh, not enough to hurt, but enough to make her jump in reaction.

She moaned and pressed her face against the bed. "I don't

know Tyson, I can't think like this. I...I want you to fuck me and let me go!"

"I'm going to fuck you Claudia," he said, his voice going impossibly deep. "I'm going to fuck you so hard you're never going to forget who owns you, who your body cries out for. You'll beg me for it long before I let you come, baby."

He continued to work his finger into her ass. The pressure increased. She panted and held as still as she could under his ministrations. She sighed in relief as he backed off only to jump when another squirt of cold jelly hit her ass. Then she felt it, some kind of object being pushed against the tight ring of her ass.

"Tyson," she asked, her voice high and uncertain. "What is it? What are you doing?"

"It's an anal plug," he answered, running his other hand soothingly across her ass cheek. "We're starting small. It's about as big as my thumb around and just about as long. You're too new to this for anything bigger, and we have a lot of work to do if I ever plan on getting in this beautiful ass."

Claudia's heart thundered and her body shivered in response as he twisted and turned the plug until she felt it slip in and the top settle between her cheeks. It felt impossibly tight.

"Just breathe, baby," he said, kissing her upraised ankle and then pressing a kiss into the palm of her hand. "You can take it. You're gorgeous and brave."

Gradually the pressure decreased as she got used to the feel of a foreign object in her ass. The visualization of what she must look like, spread out with a butt plug on display for Tyson, made her pussy grow wetter and her flesh heat in an aroused blush. "What colour is it?" she whispered, embarrassed, but wanting to know.

"Pretty pink," he said, stepping back from the bed. "Oh yeah, you look good, beautiful. Just like that."

Claudia's heart sped up as she heard him walk away from the bed. She was surprised and disappointed that he was leaving her without touching her. But she knew her punishment for running wasn't likely to end quickly. He wanted her to suffer, wondering when he would come fuck and release her. She heard the thud of his feet on the stairs.

"Tyson!" she yelled. "Don't I even get a safe word?"

She held her breath. He stopped moving, but didn't come back up the stairs. He said, "How about: I will never run away from Tyson King again? When I hear you scream those words as I'm taking that gorgeous pussy, I might consider having some mercy." He continued down the stairs, leaving her tied down doggy-style and getting wetter by the minute.

CHAPTER TWELVE

Claudia had no idea how long he left her like that. She was helpless to do anything but listen to his movements throughout the house. With the open loft she could hear him on the floor below working in the kitchen, making something to eat. She tried to think about the last time she ate and if she were hungry, but the sensations overwhelming her body were too distracting for her to worry about food.

The press of the anal plug against her tender ass had gradually morphed from uncomfortable into an incredible fullness. Every time she shifted or wiggled her ass the plug moved ever so slightly, pressing against nerve endings she didn't know existed. The feelings were intense, unexpected and so unbelievably good. The better her ass felt the more she became aware of her empty pussy and the desire to have it filled. Specifically with the fat cock of her gorgeous, overbearing captor.

Claudia bit her lip to keep from begging him to come over to the bed and fuck her. He was sitting in one of the leather chairs by the fire, and had been for a while now. She had demanded he untie her when he'd come up the stairs and sprawled out in the chair with what sounded like papers. He'd ignored her until she threatened to start screaming. Then he had calmly told her if she didn't shut up he would gag her too. Considering she was trussed up in his bed, with a butt plug buried between her ass cheeks, she decided to take him at his word and stop talking.

Unfortunately, the lack of conversation forced her to ponder the sexual heat that was nearly overwhelming her body. She had no idea simply being forced to lie naked in one spot, blind-folded, opened up and ready for Tyson's every sexual whim would make her so horny. She humped her hips against the bed a little, trying to create a little friction against her clit. She moaned in frustration when her limbs protested the movement.

More rustling caught her attention. She wondered what he was doing. If he was reading something relaxing like a newspaper or magazine, or if he brought work with him. She suspected the latter considering Tyson worked like a machine. The only time she'd heard he took off work was when he was with her.

Claudia knew exactly how to relax the big man and turn his attention away from figures and business takeovers. If she weren't tied down to a bed, she'd sashay over to him, trail her fingers across his broad, tense shoulders. Maybe give him a little massage before going around in front to stand between him and the fire. His eyes would trace over her flawless skin where the firelight caressed every generous curve. She would turn her back to him, show him what she looked like from that angle and then she'd bend over and give him a full view of her new toy. He would reach for her but she would dance away, shake her head, sending cascades of long honeyed waves dancing around her body.

She would drop to her knees on the rug, crawl up between his legs and pull his business papers out of his hands. He would let her, because he would be so distracted at this point that work would be the last thing he would want to think about. He would ease himself further down in the chair, spread his knees and beckon her closer. She would place her long feminine fingers on his thighs and pull herself up until her breasts came into his view. He would reach for her, tugging gently on her nipples while she unzipped his pants, reached in and pulled out his big, erect cock.

Claudia realized she was moaning and wriggling helplessly on the bed, pulling against the restraints in a desperate attempt to get free and make her fantasy a reality. She bit her lip to keep herself quiet, but realized that she no longer heard the rustling of papers. What she did hear was Tyson, breathing heavily and standing over her. She couldn't see him through the blindfold, but she could *feel* his presence.

"Tyson..." she pleaded.

"Beg me for it, Claudia," he rumbled, his voice sounding strained. "Tell me to fuck you harder than you've ever been fucked before. Tell me what you know I want to hear."

"Yes!" she moaned, her heart pounding and her pussy gushing at the sound of his clothes hitting the floor. "Please, fuck me Tyson, do it now. Oh god, I want you so bad."

She heard him round the end of the bed. He gripped her thighs and pulled her back toward the edge of the bed. The movement caused the roping to go tauter and her legs to spread even wider. She panted and continued to beg him mindlessly. She screamed at the unexpected invasion of his tongue as he kneeled between her thighs and licked her pussy with a ferociousness that told her he wanted her just as desperately as she wanted him. He had probably been unable to concentrate on whatever he was reading before in the chair. Instead, his heated gaze would have been drawn to her naked, bound body time and again.

"God, yes!" she keened as he suckled her labia and ran his

tongue up and down her slit, stopping to circle her clit a few times before moving up to stab his tongue into her vagina.

She was so close to exploding that her body was beginning to contract, her anal passage tightening around the plug sparking sensations all through her body. Tyson came up over her, his stomach hitting her ass, pressing against the plug. She felt him drag his penis through her folds and line up against her soaking pussy.

Claudia screamed as he slammed himself deep into her body, mercilessly driving through her contracting channel. He was so big that she could barely take him comfortably let alone with something in her ass, stretching both passages. Pain and pleasure merged into one huge crashing orgasm that swept over her like a wave. As Tyson fucked her with short, hard strokes, her orgasm went on and on. She felt fluid gush from her pussy, soaking him and easing his way.

"Fuck, baby," he snarled from behind her. "Can't hold on. So fucking good!"

She felt him as he neared his own orgasm. His thrusts became even more aggressive, her soft ass absorbing the slam of his hips. His fingers bit into her hips, holding her still as he grunted in satisfaction and came deep within her, flooding her pussy with his hot semen.

He held himself above her, his fists on the bed next to her waist, his belly flush against her ass. "Fuck. Never came that fast before."

As much as she was learning to enjoy her new toys, Claudia very much wanted to by free so she could cuddle up against the big man that had brought her mindless amounts of pleasure. "Tyson," she whispered, "can you please untie me?"

He grunted his response, but reached for her ankle. She heard a soft click and then she was free. Tyson gently pulled her leg back, massaging her thigh and calf. He gave the other

side of her body similar treatment. Claudia sighed in contentment as he cared for her. She reached up and pushed the
blindfold up her forehead, blinking sleepily in the dim light.
She rolled onto her back and watched him as he continued to
massage her body, checking her for any possible damage from
his rough treatment.

Tyson looked so beautiful to her in that moment. His big,
strong body bent over her. His dark skin contrasting sharply
with her pink flushed skin. His mahogany body looked like
black silk in the light of the fire. She sighed in disappoint-
ment when he stood and strode to the washroom, leaving her
alone on the bed. She heard him drain the tub of her previous
bath water and then run the taps, apparently filling the
whirlpool tub again. Her suspicions were confirmed when he
strode back to the bed and lifted her boneless body into his
arms.

Claudia was way too tired to even consider a protest. If
the big overly muscled man wanted to carry her around, who
was she to complain? She sighed in utter contentment as he
lowered her gently into the tub. He climbed in behind her
and tugged her into his lap. She snuggled against him and
closed her eyes, letting the feeling of repletion flood over her.
Tyson ran the bar of soap tenderly over her, caressing her as
she lolled in his arms half asleep.

He gently turned her over so her breasts her pressed
against his chest. She wrapped her arms around him and
turned her head so her face was pressed into his shoulder. He
stroked down her back until he reached her ass. With his
knees he gently nudged her legs apart. Claudia tensed,
knowing what was about to happen.

"Shhh, Claudia," he said quietly against the top of her
head. "Relax and let me take care of you."

Claudia forced the muscles of her body to gradually relax.
He squeezed her ass and gently kneaded the generous globes

until his fingers brushed against the edge of the butt plug. He continued to stroke her back and ass with one hand while the other steadily pulled the plug from her body. The heat of the water soothed away the slight sting.

He finished soaping her and then set her on the bench next to him, quickly washed himself, before emptying the tub. Standing, he picked Claudia up out of the water and stepped onto the bathmat. He set her down so she was sitting on the edge of the tub and dried her off. After drying himself, he picked her up once more.

He lowered her onto the bed and buried her in fluffy quilts before quickly removing the restraint system he had set up. After he finished tucking everything away back into the black bag he had brought in, he took his place on the bed beside her. She snuggled into his side and sighed. Her mind was still spinning with the incredible high of her orgasm. She swore she never felt so good in her entire life.

Tyson stretched his arm back and, maneuvering her pillow against his side, tucked her head into his shoulder. She snuggled against him, breathing in his scent. She slipped her arm over his stomach and pressed herself into him, feeling his hardness against her softness.

"I'm sorry I ran away, Tyson," she whispered. "I was afraid."

He didn't say anything for a second. Then he turned his head to the side and pressed a kiss against her forehead. "I know."

"You're not like him," she said.

"Go to sleep, Claudia."

Her eyes drifted shut and within minutes she was sleeping soundly, trusting her big lover to keep her safe.

CHAPTER THIRTEEN

Claudia sat on top of a boulder, her legs dangling down the side and her palms pressed back into the warm rock where the sun had heated it. She contemplated the sight of Tyson King with a fishing pole in his massive paw. She thought he never looked sexier than he did in that moment, wearing beige cargo shorts, his rippling back bared to her lascivious gaze. She might have done something about her baser inclinations if Daniel weren't standing twenty feet away from them, staring at nothing in particular and doing a good job of looking like a badass mercenary bodyguard hanging out in the woods.

She sent Daniel a glare for being himself and returned to her ponderings. She brought a leg up and studied the remnants of chipped rose coloured nail polish that had adorned her toenails. She would never have imagined that Claudia Cantore, or even Alicia Pederson, might enjoy living in the middle of nowhere, happily lost in the mountains. She still wasn't particularly fond of bears or ticks, but as long as both kept their distance she was willing to renego-tiate her previous bias against roughing it. Not that time spent in a billionaire's forest cabin could really be called roughing it.

Although she would definitely call the past week of sexy times in the arms of Tyson King 'roughing it'. Though he seemed to have forgiven her for running away from him, he was still intent on pushing her boundaries and introducing her to the kind of sex he enjoyed. She had to admit, she quickly became a very willing partner for all of his suggestions. Much to his delight. She was pretty sure he hadn't yet shown her all of his toys, but she enjoyed surprises.

Though the sex was mind-blowing and wonderful, her favourite part of their week spent together was how much he was opening up to her. He seemed to understand that if he wanted her trust then he had to give her something too. They'd finally just talked. He always liked to have her close at hand, either sitting in his lap or next to his chair so he could touch her.

Later that evening, as they once more sat together in one of Tyson's favourite positions, with Claudia cross-legged on the floor between Tyson's spread legs, his hand playing idly in her hair, he asked her, "What do you think of that gambling establishment the Sitnikov girl took you to? Would you go back there again?"

Taken aback, Claudia turned around and stared at him suspiciously. Was this a test? Was he trying to figure out if she was stupid enough to cross him and go back there on her own?

"Uh, well, first off the 'Sitnokov girl' happens to be my friend, and her name is Anya," she said firmly. She thought carefully over her impressions of the club. "No, I probably wouldn't go back there again. It was too dark, too overbearing. It felt threatening to me."

He nodded his head thoughtfully. "If you could change it to become more welcoming, what would you do?"

Anya turned around on the rug and looked up at Tyson. She had suspected before that he had plans to buy that place, but she hadn't thought too deeply into the matter. Mostly because she'd been planning on running away from him and it wouldn't have made a difference to her in the long run. She chewed on her lip and scrunched up her nose while she thought about his question, wanting to give him a good answer. She enjoyed business and would have liked to co-own Knight's Out Café if it had been a possibility with her life on the run.

"I guess... first off, I would update the interior. Get rid of some of that steel piping and add some more luxurious furnishings. A deep crimson red would look awesome with the black that's already in there. I would add some music. Something sexy, like jazz, so it would blend into the atmosphere without taking away from the lucrative gambling aspect," she explained, speaking with more conviction as she went. "I would expand the bar, make that area a little more trendy. Like, light it up from behind or something. Add some stools and tables in the bar area, as a complement to the card tables without taking away from the main point of the casino. I guess overall, make it a lot more female friendly."

"More female friendly?" he said, reaching for her and pulling her off the floor into his lap. The stack of papers he had been looking at fell unheeded. "You didn't feel welcome when you were there?"

She laughingly snorted, "You mean that one time I went and got kidnapped while I was there?"

"I prefer to call it acquired by an admirer." He grinned at her and leaned in to kiss her, his lips covering hers in a leisurely exploration. Claudia slid her arms around his neck and responded with enthusiasm. She rarely took initiative in their sexual encounters, preferring to leave the control up to him. She felt his surprise when she darted her tongue into his mouth. She retreated too quickly for his liking. With a growl, Tyson's arms wrapped around her waist and crushed her to him. He kissed her passionately, sucking her tongue into his mouth and forcing her to take more of the darting swipes he loved so much.

Finally, he released her mouth so she could take in several gasping breaths. He dipped his head to drop swift, hard kisses across her collarbone. She leaned back in his arms, giving him better access to her body. Tyson quickly disposed of her shirt and reached back to do the same with his. He swooped in to devour her bare skin, sucking her full breasts and nipples roughly into his hot mouth. Claudia moaned and arched her back, thrusting her breasts further out for his attention.

Without warning, Tyson thrust Claudia off of him, forcing her to stand on her feet. The sudden movement caused her to sway uncertainly. She understood right away when he reached out and all but tore her jean shorts from her body. She would have giggled except his hurried movements meant she was about to get fucked hard. She was starting to read him well. Today he couldn't wait to get her naked and plunge into her soaking wet pussy.

Tyson stood, towering over her. He unzipped himself and pulled his thick cock out. Without bothering to take off his pants, he picked Claudia up by the armpits and made her wrap her legs around his waist. She did, and was rewarded when he grasped her full hips and steadily pulled her down onto his towering erection. She gasped and wiggled as she was forced to accept every inch as it was thrust up into her clasping heat.

When she was fully impaled, Claudia wrapped her arms around his massive shoulders for more control and bounced herself up and then down experimentally. Tyson gritted his teeth and rumbled, "Fuck!" against the side of her head. Guessing that he liked that, Claudia did it several more times, enjoying to sensations coursing through her over-filled channel.

Of course, Tyson wasn't one to allow Claudia control for very long. He carried her, wrapped around his waist, toward the kitchen island and placed her bottom on the edge. Then he unwrapped her heels from his waist, bent her legs up until her knees were pressed against his chest and started fucking her with hard, steady strokes. This new position made the fit impossibly tight, causing Claudia to cry out and dig her short nails into his biceps. As it always was with Tyson, the bite of pain mixing with pleasure drove her relentlessly toward the peak of an intense orgasm.

"Tyson!" she screamed. "Oh god, oh fuck!"

He grunted and gripping her waist tightly, plunging ruthlessly into her with his full length. "Come for me, baby."

Claudia's orgasm exploded in an array of violent colours behind her eyelids and heavenly explosions through her pussy, which clamped down on him. The suddenly much tighter fit squeezed Tyson's cock until he couldn't hold on any longer. He picked her up off the counter and slammed her down on his cock, driving her orgasm even higher. With a shout he followed her over the edge, clamping her hips down against his and shooting jets of come inside her body.

Tyson carried her back to his chair and collapsed onto the leather seat still buried in her body. Claudia curled her legs up around him and wrapped her arms around his neck. They sat that way for a long time, just talking and gently touching each other until Tyson once more took her mouth in long, drugging kisses. He picked her up and laid her down on the rug, kicked his shorts off and crawled over top of her. He took her body with such gentleness that Claudia was swept away on a swell of the sweetest orgasm she'd ever experienced.

Tyson held her tightly in his arms, both of them silent in the glow of their mutual ecstasy. After several long moments, he stood up, towering over her prone body, and then gently lifted her up in his arms. He carried her up the stairs and tucked her in bed where she drifted off to sleep immediately with the feel of the soft, cushiony blankets surrounding her and Tyson's hard, warm body at her back. She had never felt safer.

Until the next morning.

Claudia had gotten up early when she noticed Tyson was missing from the bed. He was usually up before her, but it was still dark out and definitely earlier than usual. She climbed out from under the heavy blankets and wandered over to the loft railing. Leaning over, her blond hair streaming down, she listened for him. She heard the rumble of voices and saw a light coming from behind the kitchen in the direction of Tyson's study.

Maybe he was talking to Daniel. Though Daniel rarely stepped foot inside the house he was always around, hovering like a bird of prey, ready to strike at the slightest provocation. Just in case Tyson wasn't alone, Claudia slipped on the robe he had provided for her, purchased at a tiny boutique from a small mountain town several miles away. The silky fabric caressed her body, but covered everything important. Deciding if he didn't like her wearing stuff like this around other men then he needed to stop buying it for her, Claudia descended the stairs and padded silently to where Tyson was sitting with his back to her.

The study was as open as everything else in his home. His big cedar desk blended so well into the cabin theme, it wasn't immediately apparent this was a workspace. He was alone in the room, sitting in his expensive computer chair. Tyson was listening intently to a satellite phone placed on his desk and set on speakerphone. He didn't hear Claudia approach.

"They are looking for something the woman has," said a man's voice on the phone. "She was clever to leave with something of value. It is the reason she might live longer if they got their hands on her."

Tyson responded with a grunt and then replied, "I have what she took. My man found it at her apartment."

Claudia covered her mouth and forced herself to stand stock still behind Tyson. A wave of dizziness hit her as she imagined Mercer finding the USB key taped to the inside of her stove. Though she'd wanted to go back to get it before leaving town, she realized it wouldn't be a good idea. Her apartment would be the first place Tyson's guys would stake out when she ran.

"Have you reviewed the information?" asked the other man.

"Yes," Tyson responded immediately. "It's incriminating, enough for authorities to launch an investigation, but its not damaging enough to bury Marquez or Delgado. You're barely mentioned."

"This is good."

Claudia was surprised and dismayed that her 'evidence' hadn't been as promising as she had hoped. She hadn't been able to get past the encryptions, which was no surprise given her lack of technological expertise.

"I destroyed it," Tyson said calmly. "There are no copies."

Claudia gasped loudly smothering whatever response the other guy had given. Tyson turned to her quickly. Claudia started to back away, but he was too fast. He was out of his chair and on her in seconds. Claudia struggled against him and opened her mouth to shout at him, but his big hand settled over her lips before she could make a sound. He sat back down, with her in his lap. She heaved against him and tried to struggle out of his lap, but he held her tightly, forcing her to remain seated.

"And the woman?" asked the other man. The chill in his voice made Claudia freeze. She understood now why Tyson wanted to silence her. The other guy wasn't to know she was listening.

"She belongs to me," Tyson's voice left no room for arguments. "She never got a look at what was on the USB and while she may know enough about Marquez's operation to give evidence, she knows nothing about you, Nic."

Niccolo DeLuca! Tyson was talking to the Italian boss he had told her about. The one that was taking over Dante's operation. No wonder he wanted her to stay quiet. Claudia forced herself to relax against Tyson. She had chosen to trust him over the past week. She knew he wouldn't do anything to hurt her. As though sensing her decision, Tyson slowly lifted his hand from her mouth.

"She's all yours my friend. Congratulations *amico*, I have heard she is a beautiful woman. And also intelligent to have eluded the Miami crew for so long. She must be, to have captured your attention. I look forward to one day meeting her," Niccolo said.

Tyson smiled, his hands running over Claudia's limbs in soft strokes, soothing away her upset at overhearing such a brutal conversation. "Yes, she is that."

"I trust you can handle Marquez if he shows up in your city?" Niccolo asked.

"Of course," Tyson replied. "His escape from your Miami takeover must have been a blow."

"Yes," Niccolo said shortly.

"And you *will* take care of Delgado?" Tyson asked, an edge in his voice.

"With pleasure," Niccolo answered, his voice dangerous. "That man is a thorn in my side. I have heard he has a honey trap set up for me in Vegas. A *honey trap*, I ask you? As if that sort of thing can possibly ensnare a DeLuca."

Tyson's teeth flashed white as he grinned. "Be careful my friend, men like us, our downfall will not be bullets, but the women behind them. Perhaps you will enjoy your fall as much as I have."

The other man snorted, his voice disbelieving, "Not bloody likely."

"Take care, my friend."

"*Arrivederci*," Nic replied and then hung up.

Tyson turned immediately to Claudia, bringing her chin up so she was forced to look into his eyes. "I'm sorry I grabbed you like that, beautiful. I didn't want Nic to know you were here, he isn't ready to understand what you've become to me. To men like him, women are decorations and objects."

Claudia smiled. "I understand Tyson. I understood almost right away."

"Please don't be upset about the USB key. It had to be destroyed. I didn't want you dragged further down into this business. I should've told you, but I didn't want to argue. Not when our time here has been some of the best of my life."

"And mine," Claudia said softly, resting her head on his chest. "I trust you, Tyson. Though I would prefer you discuss things that involve me and my property."

He didn't answer. She grinned. He probably couldn't answer because the big man knew better than to lie to her. He wouldn't promise to never overstep that boundary again because he most likely would when he thought what he was doing was in her best interests. She understood him very well, maybe better than he understood himself. He was fiercely protective of her and their budding relationship. He never had a family. His mother had died young of a drug overdose and he never knew his father. He had grown up in foster care until he was able to take care of himself on the streets, when he was around thirteen. Then he had ruthlessly fought his way out of those streets and set about building the foundation for the unshakeable empire he had today.

Tyson would protect Claudia with his life, even from herself. Because she was the one thing he had that was all his. She was the one thing he had that could love him back, the way he loved her.

CHAPTER FOURTEEN

"Time to go," Daniel Mercer growled down at the two women.

Claudia tossed her long blond waves back over her shoulder and glared up at Tyson's goon. Despite spending weeks in the guy's company, he wasn't even remotely softening toward her. He acted as though she were a glass wall. A thing he could touch and guard, but also see right through. He wasn't rude, but he wasn't anything else either. It drove her nuts. It drove her to be uncharacteristically stubborn when he made suggestions she wasn't particularly fond of. Like when he *suggested* in no uncertain terms that she could meet her friend in Tyson's fortress of a penthouse rather than at a restaurant.

They had been back in the city for three days. Tyson had business to attend to and he had been unwilling to leave Claudia even for a day. She felt the same way, so she had accompanied him back. In the city, he wanted her to stay in the penthouse at all times where she was safe. In fact, he had insisted. Claudia had systematically broken him down using her ultimate methods of persuasion, which included logical argument about how careful she would be while surrounded by an army of bodyguards – and mind sizzling blowjobs. Tyson had been unable to withstand the lethal combination and had finally allowed her to go see her friend.

She opened her mouth to tell Daniel off for trying to cut short her gal pal time with Anya, who was filling her in on tons of juicy details about her champion fighter boyfriend. Much to Claudia's amusement, Anya leapt in before she could. The tiny woman stood up and went toe to toe with one of the scariest guys Claudia's imagination could conjure.

"Dude, what exactly is your problem?" Anya snapped, crossing her arms in front of her. She looked like a miniature combatant in her black studded jeans, camo tank top and signature heavy boots, blue-tipped hair brushing against her shoulder blades. "Why don't you go give cold lessons to an iceberg for a few hours? I don't even begin to understand why Ash might consider you a friend. Why don't you back off, we're talking here."

Mercer said nothing. He didn't even look down at the much shorter woman who was confronting him. He stood tall and solid next to Claudia's chair where he had posted himself for the last half hour. His imposing stature had frightened off anyone that might have approached the table in one of the city's downtown boutique restaurants. Consequently, the two women had only received water since arriving, despite the stellar online reviews. Claudia suspected her glowering ornament frightened the staff of Dockside Cafe. When she first noticed their reticence in approaching the women, Claudia had asked him politely to either sit down or go stand by the door so they could talk in peace. Without a word he had declined both suggestions.

"What exactly is your problem? You're a bodyguard, as in

you *guard* her *body*," Anya demanded and pointed at Claudia. "You don't get to dictate when we're done here. We'll let you know when we're ready to go. Now why don't you do us a favour and go be a good statue over there."

Daniel tilted his head down, studying the annoying woman with quiet menace, like a cobra judging the best moment to strike. Claudia jumped to her feet, inserting herself between the two of them, disliking the extra chilling glint that had come into Daniel's eyes. She had no doubt he was picturing all the ways he could dispose of Anya's small body.

Anya poked her head around Claudia's arm and glared up at him. "I know people," she said, drawing a finger across her throat for emphasis.

Claudia stifled a laugh and quickly turned to hug Anya. "It's been great seeing you again, Anya. Let's do it again sometime, *after* I have a chat with Tyson about boundaries."

Still glaring fireballs up at Daniel, Anya hugged the taller woman back and mumbled, "Dogs without manners."

Daniel took a step forward, hooked Claudia by the arm and pulled her out of Anya's grip, texting the driver that they were on their way out. Claudia waved at Anya, hoping she didn't look too much like a woman being abducted from a popular restaurant. She stood stiffly in Daniel's grip as he led her out onto the sidewalk and whisked her into the car with a hand on top of her head to protect her from the frame. Slamming the door shut he got into the front passenger side, next to the driver.

Claudia was reminded sharply of the first night she met Tyson King. Of how he had taken her forcefully out of the gambling club he was now buying and pushed her into his vehicle. She had been so terrified that he was planning on handing her over to Dante and Franco. The memory made her temper soar even more, so she wasn't particularly careful when she spoke to Daniel.

"What exactly gives you the right to dictate to me," she demanded, smacking the back of his seat with frustration. "Do you get off on humiliating women? Because if so, congratulations, mission accomplished. You made me feel like a child back there, incapable of making my own decisions. You treated me like I can't even walk by myself!"

Claudia expected Daniel's customary reaction of not reacting at all. So she was surprised when he shifted in his seat, turned his bearded jaw toward her and stared at her like he might a particularly annoying bug. "You have no idea what gets me off, little girl, so don't talk about things you don't understand. If it amused me to humiliate you, trust me, you wouldn't be able to sit for a month. In my opinion, you can't walk by yourself, talk by yourself or do anything without getting yourself into trouble. You belong to the boss and that makes you my responsibility."

Claudia gasped and pushed back in her seat until her spine moulded against the leather. It wasn't far enough away. She could still feel the ever-present menace radiating from his skin. Such a contrast from his big, sexy boss. Tyson could be scary, but his adoration for her cancelled out his terrifying demeanour. She wished in that moment that she were with Tyson, safe in his arms.

"Don't talk to me that way," Claudia said, trying to sound angry.

Daniel just looked through her, replying, "Stop acting like a child," before turning back to face the front of the car.

They didn't take the car elevator up, instead coming to a halt in front of the huge luxury apartment complex. Daniel was in the process of giving instructions to Mike, the driver, when Claudia decided she'd had about all of Daniel Mercer's oppressive presence that she could handle. She reached for the door handle and opened it.

Daniel quickly turned in his seat and snapped, "Stay put and wait for me."

"Bite me," Claudia snapped back, standing up on the sidewalk in her three-inch Saint Laurent heels and slammed the door shut. She glared swiftly at Daniel as he hurriedly finished his conversation with Mike and reached to open the door.

Claudia reached for the swinging door of the lobby and entered the richly furnished, air-conditioned room. She automatically turned to smile at the concierge on her way to the elevators when she noticed he was missing from his post, which was highly unusual. Apprehension tingled up and down her spine as Claudia hesitantly approached the big marble reception desk. Peeking over the top, she saw him.

Her mouth opened in a soundless scream. Her hand automatically came up to cover her gaping mouth. The regular concierge, an older man named Oscar, was laying flat on his back, eyes open in a sightless stare. There was a hole in his forehead, with burn marks around it where someone had shot him point blank. Claudia backed away, gasping for Daniel. Her shocked gaze met his, pleading for help, as he stepped into the lobby. His usual stoic expression turned to concern at her white face and glassy eyes. His sharp eyes swept the lobby.

Just as Claudia was about to tell him about the dead man, the door separating the lobby from the main floor garage banged open and two men holding semi-automatic rifles stepped through. Daniel acted so swiftly Claudia didn't even have time to process who they might be. He lunged toward her, hooked her around the waist with a thick arm and jumped over the concierge desk, turning as he went to keep his back to the guys who were just realizing their prey was in the building.

Claudia landed hard on the floor next to the dead concierge with a very heavy Daniel landing on top of her. She groaned at the impact, but bit her lip so Daniel could effectively do his job without worrying about her. He rolled off of her, coming up in a crouch and pulling a gun out of the shoulder holster hidden under his jacket. Claudia whimpered and covered her head when a spray of bullets hit the marble desk, raining chunks of stone and wood down on their heads.

Daniel returned fire from the side of the desk, telling them without words that it was in their best interests to keep their distance. Silence followed as she heard them take cover behind the marble pillars that ran the length of the lobby. One of them shouted, "Give us the woman and you walk, Mercer."

Daniel snorted and laughed coldly, replying with a gruff shout, "If you know my name, then you know that's not going to happen. Leave now, and I'll give you a head start before I go hunting."

A burst of gunfire answered his deadly statement. Daniel returned fire while Claudia huddled next to him, the hem of her skirt brushing against the dead guy on the floor next to her. She held herself stiffly and wondered if she was going to get out of this situation alive. They had asked for her, which indicated they might want her alive. She wasn't sure 'alive' was a good way to be if they were planning on taking her to Dante or Franco. She had to force herself not to clutch Daniel. He needed space if he was going to defend them.

The gunfire stopped for a few seconds. The ding of the elevator sounded deafening in the silence of the lobby. The elevators were directly to the right of her and Daniel's position. If another gunman stepped out, they'd have a clean line of sight, unimpeded by the reception desk. If it was a resident, they would probably die. Claudia held her breath and then moaned in distress as a young woman stepped off the elevator. She wore a floor length skirt under a jean jacket. Her long dark hair swept down her back in gorgeous disarray. She couldn't be older than twenty-five.

The woman was holding a walking stick, too. Dear god, was she blind? Claudia was about to scream out to her when the woman, apparently instinctively, dropped to her knees and then rolled over on her side, covering her head. A spray of bullets hit the metal doors of the closing elevator right where the woman had been standing. Claudia turned to Daniel to warn him about the innocent woman.

He was staring toward the other woman, a look of anger and horror frozen on his face. Claudia had never seen such emotion penetrate his deadly exterior. Did he know the other woman? From her current position, Claudia doubted it. The woman looked soft and feminine, the opposite of anything that might attract Daniel Mercer. Yet, he was watching her like a hawk watches over its young. Deadly, uncannily still, ready to strike if necessary.

Thinking quickly, Claudia said, "Give me one of those guns."

Daniel looked down to where Claudia was crouched under him. Her green eyes held his earnestly. Like most people, she usually dropped her eyes from him and looked away. But this time she meant it and she wouldn't back down from him. He ignored her request. Apparently his job was to protect her, not listen to her.

"Shut up," Daniel replied, his eyes searching out the other woman. She was still cowering against the wall next to the elevator bank. Her walking stick had fallen and rolled a few feet away from her when she hit the floor. She was curled on her side, her arms over her head. As though that could save her from bullets.

"Please, Daniel!" Claudia said, touching his arm. "I can shoot, and if we don't do something, she'll die."

Daniel growled at her and she dropped her hand as if burned. Claudia wished she could make him listen. Now was not the time for him to be the misogynistic jerk that was her usual deadly shadow. She needed him to listen so they could save the blind woman who was helpless against a hail of bullets!

A scream snapped their attention back to her. A spray of bullets just over her head rained chunks of wall down on her. Claudia's heart sped into overtime. They had to do something, before the young woman was killed! It was most likely Claudia's fault the woman was in danger. She had little doubt these gunmen belonged to Franco Delgado, whose pockets and reach were equally deep. Without putting much thought into her actions (or she would never have dared), Claudia hauled her fist back and punched Daniel in the arm.

"Ouch!" Claudia wailed.

Daniel looked down at her in surprise. Claudia shook her aching hand and glared at him in annoyance. He could at least look a tiny bit injured. Or like he even noticed she had just punched him. Instead he looked mildly confused. *Well, here goes,* thought Claudia reaching for the other gun still in Daniel's holster, *think Anya and let's do this shit.* Before he could react, Claudia launched herself around the side of the desk closest to the outside doors and started shooting at the marble pillars containing bad guys.

Daniel looked shocked for a split second as he realized Claudia had swiped one of the guns. She feared he would reach out and snatch her back rather than go after the terrified blind woman.

"Go get her!" Claudia snapped, trying to infuse as much command into her voice as she could manage.

Used to acting quickly, Daniel didn't say another word. He

took the questionable cover fire she was laying down and dove for other woman. The shooters were focusing mainly on their target, Claudia, and trying not to get shot by her. It became quickly obvious they were trying to pin her down without killing her. Daniel ran in a crouch and swooped the other girl up into his arms. Her terrified shriek drew the shooters' attention back to him.

"Motherfucker!" Daniel snarled, taking a hit in the back.

Claudia felt sick and desperately hoped he was wearing his usual armour underneath his jacket. She flung her arm around the side of the desk and squeezed off several more shots, trying to lay cover so Daniel could get back to the relative safety of the big reception desk. The attackers responded by shooting all around her again without actually getting too close to her position.

Using his body to protect the terrified woman in his arms, Daniel dove for cover behind the concierge desk. "You're safe," he said in his gruff voice, dropping the terrified woman and using his weapon to draw fire back to himself.

"Get your ass back here," he snapped at Claudia.

Relieved that Daniel and the woman were safe once more, Claudia crawled back toward him, her hair swinging wildly around her face. When she reached his side, Daniel snatched his gun from her shaking hand, checked the chamber and shoved her down next to the other woman. Claudia went willingly, happy to relinquish control to the big bodyguard once more.

"Are you hurt?" Claudia asked the woman, touching her shoulder gently. When she flinched away, Claudia said soothingly, "I'm not going to hurt you."

"Wh... what's happening?" The woman asked, pushing dark curls off her face and sitting up with Claudia's help. Her blank, brown eyes reflected her confusion and terror.

"We're being shot at," Claudia answered quickly.

"I'm blind, not stupid. I figured that much out from the shooting sounds!" She snapped back. "Why are we being shot at in what's supposed to be one of the most secure and safe buildings in the city? Tyson King lives here, for the love of god! This place should be a fortress."

Claudia blinked in surprise and then smiled involuntarily. The woman had spunk, which Claudia could appreciate. She reminded Claudia a little of Anya. "I'm Claudia, Tyson's... girlfriend," she supplied. "And the guy that grabbed you is Daniel Mercer, Tyson's head of security. If anyone can keep us safe until help arrives it's him."

She conveniently left out the part where it was her fault they were sitting in a shooting range. Her desperate gaze lifted to Daniel, silently begging him to save them. Daniel looked back, his eyes hooded, expression grave. Claudia had put her arm around the other woman to protect and comfort the blind girl. The woman seemed to accept the embrace, clutching Claudia back.

Finally she spoke, her voice shaking a little. "My name is Addie... Addie Sterling."

"Hi Addie," Claudia said into her ear over the sound of gunfire. "It's nice to meet you."

The absurdity of their polite meeting hit both women and they laughed together quietly crouched on the floor. Claudia was busy reassuring Addie as best she could when Daniel's sharp gaze swivelled to the right, toward the elevator bank. Claudia followed his line of sight and watched in horror as two men burst through the stairwell door next to the elevators. The three of them were completely vulnerable where they were crouched, not even hidden from that angle.

Luckily Daniel saw the men before they had time to register the trio. He ruthlessly took them out where they stood. Both bodies hit the floor, one right after the other. Daniel shouted at two more men that came hurtling out of the stairwell. Claudia stiffened in terror before she recognized them. They were Daniel's men, and by extension Tyson's! The tension left her as the two used the doorway for cover and shot up the marble pillars, forcing the remaining gunmen to flee. In a matter of seconds, the entire ordeal was ended. The gunmen covered each other until they could reach the main doors and run for safety now that they were outnumbered.

Daniel stood, taking Claudia's arm and forced her to her feet. She yelped and stumbled, dropping her arms from Addie. The other woman lay on the floor, pushing herself up by her arms and staring blankly around in confusion.

"Daniel!" Claudia gasped, bracing herself against him. She hastily removed her hand when his icy eyes swept her with chilling intensity.

"Is the penthouse still secure?" Mercer asked his men.

"Yeah, I think so," muttered the closest one. "We caught these bastards on their way up. They had equipment to break through the reinforced stairwell door, but didn't get that far."

"Good. Take her upstairs," he snapped, shoving Claudia at Brandon, one of the other bodyguards. "King is on his way, he'll want to see her safe. Stay with her until he arrives. Sweep the penthouse for good measure."

Turning to Theo, he said, "Stay for the police report. Give only the necessary information. They can talk to me if they have a problem. Have the rest of our guys sweep the building. I'll be with Miss Sterling in her apartment, suite 1210."

Claudia stumbled a little as Brandon forced her to step around a dead body. Claudia was beginning to wonder if being an unbearable asshole was a prerequisite for becoming a bodyguard. She also wondered how the heck Daniel knew where Addie Sterling lived. Did he memorize everyone in the building for potential threats?

"I'm not going anywhere with you," Addie snapped

crossly, earning a smile from Claudia as Brandon pulled her past them. She reached out and gave Addie's limp hand a quick squeeze.

"I heard what you said to that other guy. You know where I live, which under any other circumstances would make me extremely uncomfortable. But since I just survived some kind of wild west showdown, I'm just going to be grateful for my life and not question why you seem to know my name and apartment number. But I'll thank you to leave me the hell alone. I don't know you and I don't trust you."

Claudia craned her head to hear the rest of what Addie was saying to Daniel. She wanted to cheer for the other woman and tell her to give the guy hell. Another part of her wanted to warn the woman to tread carefully since she couldn't see the extent of Daniel Mercer's icy, terrifying demeanor. At the moment his visage was decidedly more grim than usual.

The last thing Claudia saw was Daniel reach for the other woman and say in a growl, "You're coming with me."

The elevator doors closed behind Claudia and Brandon. Claudia yanked her arm out of his steely grip and glared at him. "Why don't you guys make it easier for a woman to appreciate your protection?"

Brandon looked over at Claudia. He was about the same height as her, but thickly muscled. He shrugged and answered, "We don't get paid to make nice with the boss' woman. Just save her ass when it gets shot at."

Claudia shot him a look and crossed her arms in front of her. "Is that right? I bet if I asked Tyson, he'd make you guys smile for me."

His face finally cracked in a half grin. "Probably. But you ain't going to do that."

"And why is that?"

"Because bodyguards are more effective and sexier when

we're being serious and menacing," he said completely serious.

Claudia laughed as the elevator arrived at the penthouse suite. The doors slid open with a ding. She looked up into the face of Dante Marquez. He was holding a handgun out and it was trained on her head. Her mirth fled as she turned anguished eyes on Brandon who was reaching for his gun. Before he could get it out of the holster Dante shot him in the head. Blood sprayed across the elevator, splattering across Claudia's white skirt, Brandon hit the floor of the elevator, dead.

Dante tucked his gun into his pants and reached for Claudia. She balled her hand up into a fist and sent it flying into his jaw, hoping to distract him enough to run past him and make it into the penthouse.

The hit wasn't hard enough. It only swung his head to the side. He turned back to her, his black gaze cold and merciless. He retaliated swiftly, striking Claudia in the side of the head with so much force she was knocked right off her feet and into the side panel of the elevator. He grabbed her arm before she could slide to the ground and held her tightly.

Claudia whimpered and reached out to brace herself against the wall, her head swimming unbearably. She put a hand over her cheek and ear where he had struck her. The skin was numb to her gentle touch. She could feel heat flushing her skin. She had been stupid to attack him. Now he would probably kill her faster.

Dante hauled her off the elevator, over Brandon's limp body and dragged her bodily down the hall to the door of the penthouse. He threw her into the door and growled, "Open it."

Claudia thought about denying him entry to the penthouse. Once she entered the door code it would also disarm the alarm panel. There was a panic button on the panel that

Tyson had shown her. Dante was arrogant but he wasn't stupid. He would know what she was doing. She decided to give him what he wanted, hopefully buying herself a few more minutes in the process. If Tyson could reach her in time he would tear the murdering bastard apart with his bare hands. She entered the code for the penthouse and staggered helplessly as Dante strode in with her in tow.

CHAPTER FIFTEEN

"I've missed you, Alicia."

Claudia stared in shock and horror as she stumbled into Tyson's living room. Dante Marquez, her ex-boyfriend, surveyed the room as if he owned the place. He looked the same as he had when she'd last seen him a year and a half ago. He was a few inches shorter than her in her expensive heels. His chest and shoulders were leanly muscled. His tanned skin and black hair attested to his Cuban ancestry. He was a handsome man, with dark eyes, a sharp nose and high cheekbones.

Though she despised him with every part of her, she also saw the original appeal. Claudia had spent months agonizing over the stupidity of her decisions. In the face of Dante's commanding presence and good looks, it was a miracle any woman could resist him. Until they saw the darkness that lurked within. It hadn't taken Claudia long to discover his true colours. She wondered how many other women had found out too late.

"Dante," she said quietly.

He turned to her, studying her striking features in minute detail as though memorizing her. Claudia's heart sped up as he reached for her, taking her hand in a hard grip and forcing her to step into the heat of his body. She stiffened at the feel of her soft breasts meeting his hard shoulder. He wrapped his arms around her and held her loosely in his embrace, his eyes searching her face and body.

"Being a rich man's whore looks good on you, Alicia."

Claudia shuddered when he pushed his nose under her ear and nuzzled her jaw. "My name is Claudia now," she said defiantly.

He breathed in her scent and started rocking her as though dancing. Claudia stumbled against him, the adrenalin from the gunfight, the shock from Brandon's pointless death and the blow to her head conspiring to drain all of the energy from her body. His arms tightened around her and he continued to rock her against him, drawing a hand over her shoulder and smoothing it down the cascade of soft, wavy hair. Claudia shuddered in his grip, wanting nothing more than to break away from him, but fearing what her unpredictable ex would do if she shoved him away.

"You will always be my Alicia," he murmured into her hair. "The only pussy to make me want her so bad I was willing to deal with Delgado. You've embarrassed me where he's concerned, Alicia. I'm afraid he wants me to torture you for that thing you took and then get rid of you."

She shuddered again, her breath catching in her throat. "Tyson is on his way, Dante. He's a powerful man. He won't enjoy finding you here in his home, touching his woman."

Dante nodded against her shoulder, still holding her tightly. "That's what I was planning on. We knew eventually he would show himself. The big man himself, drawn out of hiding. He'll discover his favourite possession is missing."

Claudia frowned, still stumbling to keep up with Dante's disjointed movements. "Why would you want him to find you? He's going to kill you when he finds you here. Just go, you still have time to get away."

Dante finally stopped moving and pushed Claudia back a few steps. He looked into her beautiful face, reached out to touch the cheek that was beginning to darken in a bruise. Claudia should have been prepared for the blow. She had known it was coming from the moment she set eyes on her arrogant ex-boyfriend.

His fist hit her square in the stomach, dropping Claudia instantly to the floor. Her arms came around her middle as if to protect herself. Her face strained with the effort to draw in air and gag at the same time. Spots swam in her vision as she slowly lost the fight to get much needed oxygen into her lungs.

Dante bent over her, taking a fist full of her long hair and bringing her face up to his. "I've been waiting and watching, you little bitch, for the opportunity to get my hands on you again. I was going to do what Delgado wanted, torture and kill you."

Claudia moaned as he once more dropped his head into the crook of her shoulder and bit down hard on the tender skin. "But I find I still want a piece of this ass again before I slit that pretty throat." He dropped his hand and squeezed the globe of her ass cheek viciously, drawing a pained yelp from the woman under him.

Still hunched down in front of her, Dante pulled a radio off his belt and said, "Marquez here, where's my ride at?"

A crackling reply answered, "ETA ten minutes."

Dante leered down at her, menace twisting his good looks. "I think I'll fuck you in his bed. We'll find out how much he wants for my sloppy seconds. I'd rather deal with money than shit like Delgado. Now that Miami is closed, I can use the extra cash."

Dante dragged her up by the hair. Claudia reached out to

grab the counter for balance, but he yanked her back into his arms, crushing her in a painful embrace. His lips found hers, caressing her gently. Dante had always been cruel that way. Keeping her on edge with his gentleness, wondering when he might turn on her in a rage.

"You're delusional if you think Tyson won't kill you for this," Claudia gasped, trying to push him away.

Dante bit down on her lip drawing blood. Claudia cried out, her hand flying up to her mouth. She felt a trickle of blood flow down her chin from the cut. "He can't touch me, bitch. I have his woman, and I have Delgado at my back. If Tyson King lays a hand on me, he's a dead man."

Claudia tried desperately to reason with him as he began dragging her to the back of the penthouse, toward the stairs that lead up to the bedroom. "You're underestimating Tyson, Dante. He won't tolerate this. He's a possessive man and he's going to lose his shit when he finds out you've touched me. I also think you're overestimating Franco Delgado. From what I've heard, he only cares about his Vegas interests."

He pulled her up the spiral staircase with a hand twisted in her hair. Claudia clutched at the railing trying to keep her balance. He wasted no time with his ten-minute limit. Claudia suspected he planned on leaving the penthouse with her when his ride arrived. She hoped he couldn't do too much damage in that time and prayed that Tyson arrived before Dante could leave with her.

When they reached the top of the stairs and entered the bedroom, Dante flung Claudia around so she was facing him. "I've been watching you with him, Claudia. I know exactly how you like it." He reached out and took a fist full of her blouse in each hand, tearing the delicate fabric easily and yanking it off of her.

"I've seen him buy things for you," he said, reaching out for her and turning her in his arms. He pressed his chest against her bare back and whispered in her ear while yanking the zipper down on her skirt and pushing the material off her hips. "I know he's been giving it to you in the ass. Didn't know you were into that kinky shit, or I'd've gone there first."

She shivered in fear as she stood wearing only her white bra and thong set and a pair of high heels. He pushed her in front of him, walking her awkwardly toward the bed. Claudia resisted, but he held her tightly, pinned against his body. He grabbed a fistful of her long blond hair and shoved her face down onto the bed. He kicked her knees apart, forcing a cry of pain from her. Bent over her with one knee on the bed, hand still in her hair, he breathed into her neck. He reached down and ran his hand roughly over her bare ass cheek, shoving a rough finger into the crotch of her panties.

"Fuck you!" she mumbled into the bedding.

"That's the plan, bitch," he snarled, shoving his erection into her hip and fingering her body roughly. "I plan on taking this little asshole, just the way you like it. I'll tear you apart, make you remember what it's like to be fucked by me."

Claudia wanted to cry. She hated that he was going to have sex with her right there on the same bed she and Tyson made love on. That he was going to take her in a place no man had been yet. She wanted Tyson to be her first and last. She wanted him now with an overwhelming desperation. She wanted to tell him she loved him.

The last thought leant her a burst of strength as she bucked against Dante throwing him off enough for her to bring a leg up and give him a strong mule kick to the crotch. Her aim was slightly off and she got him in the top of the thigh, but the lethal heel she wore added enough emphasis that he felt the kick clear through his groin.

Dante flung himself off of her, standing up behind her prone body. "Fuck, you stupid little bitch, you nearly got me in the balls!" His retribution was predictably brutal. He punched her in the back above her kidney. Claudia slid off the bed in agony and would have curled up in a ball on the floor, but he caught her face in a vicious backhand.

She was saved from worse by the crackling of his radio. "Bird's here. It's time to go."

Dante pulled it off his belt and snapped, "We'll be right out."

He reached down and grabbed her arm. "Get up," he snapped, ignoring her pained cry when he yanked her onto the feet.

Claudia swayed and nearly fainted. Blackness engulfed her, causing her knees to collapse out from under her. With a vicious curse, Dante tossed her roughly over his shoulder. She screamed out in pain when her abused belly hit his hard flesh and stretched her back where he had punched her. She wondered how much more she could take.

He strode quickly out onto the balcony with her and looked around. He took another set of stairs two at a time to the roof of the penthouse where a helicopter was in the process of landing. Claudia's brain was starting to disassociate from her body thanks to the sheer amount of abuse she had experienced in the past hour. She idly wondered how she hadn't noticed Tyson had a helicopter pad before now. She should have assumed, after seeing his fancy car elevator.

Her hair tangled around her head from the blades as the helicopter landed. Dante ran forward and tossed her into the machine, climbing in behind her. The helicopter immediately began to ascend. Thoughts collided in Claudia's head as she pondered the incredible illegality of what was happening to her and how there didn't seem to be much concern for safety as the helicopter took off with its door open and the passengers unseatbelted.

"Tyson!" she gasped as Tyson, Mercer and several of their men ran out onto the pool deck with guns drawn. Claudia stood up, reaching out as though to touch the man she loved, even though he was twenty feet below her and getting farther away. Dante was in her way, but she didn't care, she pressed forward trying to get around his legs.

The helicopter moved from the pad, over the outdoor patio and pool toward the edge of the building. The water of the pool was whipped into waves by the movement of the helicopter blades. Tyson stared up at Claudia and Dante with such deadly intensity she almost felt sorry for Dante. Tyson was going to tear him apart limb from bloody limb.

"Sit down, you fucking bitch," Dante snarled turning to her.

Claudia stared back at him and then made a split second decision that she hoped wasn't the last she would make. She lunged past Dante and launched herself out the door, hoping the pool was deep enough that she wouldn't kill herself. Or possibly hit the edge or go over the side of the fifty-story building, because she never had been good at aiming. Dante grabbed her wrist as she flew past him. Her momentum carried her forward, nearly hurtling her head first out the door.

"Claudia, no!" Tyson bellowed from below.

She stared down at Tyson and reached for him as Dante stood to get his arms around her waist and haul her back into the helicopter. Claudia twisted around in Dante's arms and threw her arms around his neck, surprising him into loosening his grip. Her long hair flew around them, binding them together. She smiled at him, giving him a bloody grin from where he had split her lip and pushed her heeled feet into the seat as hard as she could, launching them both backwards into the air.

CHAPTER SIXTEEN

It was amazing to Claudia how long a split second could feel when a person was castigating themselves for making a very bad decision. She screamed in terror, her arms still locked around Dante's neck, as she fell through the air, hoping desperately that pool tiles didn't hurt too much after a thirty-foot fall. They missed the tiles and hit the pool together, the force of their entry driving them to the bottom. Claudia bent her knees, but the impact was minimal. She let go of Dante's neck and pushing her feet against the concrete bottom, propelling herself back up.

Claudia broke through the water gasping for air and looked around in confusion, water streaming over her head and into her eyes. She immediately turned to where Tyson was frantically calling her name and started swimming weakly toward him. Dante surfaced in front of her and, immediately taking in the disadvantage of his situation, surrounded by an extremely angry Tyson King and his men, grabbed Claudia.

She struggled in his grip, which caused his weight to drive her under the water repeatedly. She hoped Tyson could get to her before Dante managed to drown her. A shot hit the water next to her and Dante's grip loosened. She surfaced and shoved him away causing him to scream out in pain. He was clutching his shoulder, blood pouring through his fingers into the water around them.

"Claudia, baby," Tyson said from next to her. "Hold on to me."

Claudia turned and immediately floated into the safety of Tyson's massive arms. He had jumped into the pool and was coming to her rescue when someone had shot Dante. She guessed the shooter was Daniel, who was in the process of pulling a struggling, shouting Dante from the pool. Daniel looked over at Claudia and her battered face and clamped a cruel hand over Dante's wound. Dante screamed in agony.

"Aw," Claudia said weakly, resting her head on Tyson's big shoulder and letting him swim her to safety, "I think he likes me a tiny bit better now."

Tyson pushed her up by the waist into waiting hands. She was quickly wrapped in a towel, covering her body, which was clad in nothing but now transparent bra and panties. Unable to stand, she sat with her legs curled underneath her on the deck tiles, which were warm from the sun overhead. Tyson hauled himself out of the pool. His white shirt had come open and water poured off of his bared chest and suit pants.

He hunched down in front of Claudia, taking her battered face gently into the massive palm of his hand. Turning it left and right, he examined her with fierce eyes. "You've been hurt," he said, his calm voice belying the fury she knew vibrated through him.

"I'm okay," she mumbled tiredly, touching his fingers and pressing her hand against his where it rested on her face.

He reached out and pulled her towel away. "Tyson!" she gasped looking around to see if anyone was watching her. Tyson's men had wisely occupied their gazes elsewhere while he continued his examination. He touched her stomach and then turned her over and ran his big hands down her back. Claudia gritted her teeth and braced her palms against the deck tiles when his fingers grazed the tender spot over her right kidney.

"Son-of-a-bitch!" Tyson thundered above her. Claudia looked over her shoulder startled. "He used you like a fucking punching bag."

Claudia turned over and looked up into Tyson's face. The anguish reflected there startled her. She knew he would be angry that Dante had touched her, Tyson's woman, his possession. But she hadn't imagined that Tyson would feel the hurt on her behalf. Suddenly she realized he felt helpless in the face of her terror and pain.

She touched the bulge of his muscular forearm where it was braced on the ground next to her bare hip. "Tyson," she whispered, "look at me."

He did. His dark eyes bored into her pained green ones. "Look at me," she repeated, reaching up to touch his hard jaw. "I'm here, I'm alive. He hurt me, but nothing permanent."

Tyson nodded, brushing his stubbled jaw against her small fingers. He turned his head and captured her fingers in his, pressing a kiss into the palm of her hand. Finally he looked down into her eyes and said, "A part of me died when you jumped out of that helicopter, Claudia. I've never been so afraid in my life."

She nodded and snuggled into his chest. He let her draw comfort from him for a minute before setting her away. He reached down and took her heels off one at a time, tenderly, the way he had the first night when he brought her to his penthouse against her will. Then he picked up the white deck towel and tucked it around her shivering body before turning to Mike, who was standing near them. "Take her inside and warm her up. Don't let her come out here."

"But Tyson..." Claudia reached for him. He pushed her

hand away, picked her up off the deck and handed her to Mike, who took her weight into his arms. "Please Tyson, I don't want you to hurt him."

Tyson didn't say anything. His face was set in deadly lines, his eyes merciless. He backed up a couple of steps and turned away, saying to another of his men, "Go inside with them and help keep an eye on her. She doesn't need to see this and she might try to get past Mike."

The guy nodded and followed her and Mike into the penthouse. Claudia recognized the futility of trying to talk to Tyson. He was angrier than she'd ever seen him, angrier than maybe he'd ever been before. He wasn't about to show Dante mercy. Not that Claudia thought Dante deserved any, but she didn't want Tyson to kill the man. She wanted justice, but she didn't want anyone to die because of her.

Claudia choked back a sob when she heard a crack and a terrified scream before Mike strode into the penthouse with her tucked safely in his arms. She buried her face in his shirt and let him carry her upstairs to the bedroom. There he tried to place her on the bed, but Claudia immediately scrambled off shaking her head. Her legs still wouldn't hold her, so she backed away from the bed on her hands and knees.

She didn't realize she was crying until she felt the tears splash over her chest. She swiped at them with a hand and huddled on the floor crying in misery and shock. Mike took the room in at a glance, saw the tattered clothes she had been wearing earlier and, with a swear, knelt swiftly at her side.

"Okay, *chica*," he said softly, pulling her into his strong arms. "You don't have to go on the bed right now. Why don't we get you into the shower and warm you up?"

Claudia, who was shivering violently, nodded her head and allowed him to lift her again and carry her into the bathroom. He set her gently on the vanity while he turned the shower on and tested the heat. He turned back to her, scrubbing a hand over his head and looking both shy and awkward at the same time. The look on the big, tough bodyguard-driver nearly brought a smile to Claudia's lips. He had no idea what to do with a battered woman that had suffered several traumas in the course of an hour.

"I can manage," she said softly, pushing herself off the vanity and forcing herself to stand on wobbly legs.

Mike looked skeptical, but he turned toward the bathroom door in relief. "Okay. You go ahead and get in the water and warm up. I'll be right here in the bedroom with the door open. Call if you need me."

"Mike," she said, stopping him. "Are they going to kill him?" she asked bleakly.

He looked back at her, clearly weighing his words. After a moment he said, "They're doing to him what any one of us would do to a man that hurt someone we love."

Claudia nodded, "So, that's a yes?"

Mike left without answering. Claudia sighed and decided now wasn't the time to examine her ethics too closely. If someone had threatened Tyson in the same way, she knew exactly how she would retaliate. Claudia dropped the towel, stripped out of her bra and panties with clumsy fingers and walked shakily into the shower. Unable to continue standing, she allowed her body to collapse gently against the stone tiles until her bare butt was on the floor of the shower. She pulled her knees up, wrapped her arms around her legs and dropped her head. She sat that way for a long time, letting the feel of the water soothe away the chill both inside and outside of her body.

Tyson found her like that. Mike had told him about the scene in the bedroom. He had listened and stared down at the remnants of the clothes that had been torn from his woman's body. He wanted to kill Dante all over again. Then he wanted to kill anyone that associated with Dante. And he would. One at a time, until the Miami underworld knew exactly who Tyson King was and why his woman was untouchable.

"Claudia," he said softly, bending down in front of her.

She brought her head up fast, startled. Fear flashed across her face and she tensed as though readying herself for another battle. "Shhh," Tyson said soothingly. He reached up and shut the shower off. "It's just me."

The fear receded, replaced with wariness as she asked, "Is it over, is he..."

Tyson just looked at her, answering her without words. She nodded and started to get up. He reached for her and pulled her out of the shower stall and into his arms. Reaching behind him, he pulled a fresh, fluffy towel off the rack and wrapped it around her. She sighed and relaxed into him. Tyson held her tightly, absorbing her entire weight against himself.

"I have to ask you something," he rumbled against the top of her head.

"Mmmhmm..." she answered, swaying against him. Her eyes closed with fatigue.

"Did he rape you?"

Claudia stiffened against him. She brought her head up slowly and examined his eyes. She didn't see disgust, only the same anguish she had seen outside when he was examining her injuries.

Shaking her head she said, "He didn't have time."

"But he was going to?" Tyson asked, his face rigid.

With a sigh she answered him truthfully. "Yes, he intended to sodomize me. He wanted to hurt me bad and probably would have done it if the helicopter hadn't arrived."

Tyson's entire body was now rigid against her. She ran her hands over his huge arms soothingly and said, "I'm okay now,

Tyson. He didn't get the chance to do any irreparable damage."

Tyson shook his head, his eyes filled with rage and sorrow. "He did," he said, tapping gentle fingers against her forehead. "This is something you should have been protected from. You'll never forget how you felt today."

Claudia chewed on her lip for a second wondering what she could say. "He was always going to get to me Tyson. He was determined and he was patient. He's been tracking me for over a year. If you hadn't come along when you did, he would have found me alone and unprotected. Maybe I'll remember this day, and maybe I'll have a few nightmares. But I'll also remember that you saved my life. Not just from Dante, but from my life on the run."

Tyson looked at her intently, absorbing her words. Finally he reached down and picked her up off the floor as gently as he could, mindful of the bruising on her back and stomach. He carried her into the bedroom and placed her on the bed. With Tyson there she didn't feel the same overwhelming fear she had earlier. The ragged clothes had been removed and their bedroom looked normal. She snuggled into the bedding as he stripped his clothes off and joined her on the bed.

He pulled her into his embrace, treating her with such delicacy that she wanted to weep. He pushed the wet strands of hair off her forehead and kissed her gently. "Claudia, I'm in love with you. I have been from the first moment I saw your smile and wished it were mine. Please, be my wife. I want to share everything with you in this life. I want to give you every gift you can imagine, take you on trips and show you the world. I want you at my side, always."

Claudia smiled widely and reached out to touch his lips as though capturing the words forever. "Yes," she whispered. "I'll marry you, Tyson King. I want to be your bride. I love you too. I wanted to tell you when I thought I would die today. That's why I jumped out of the helicopter. Because I couldn't stand the thought of flying away from you without knowing if I would see you again."

"Never," he said fiercely. "You will *never* leave me again. We're forever, Claudia King."

CHAPTER SEVENTEEN

"These just arrived for you."

Claudia looked up and smiled as Laney Paul walked into her office. The smaller woman set a box on her desk and took a step back. She was about 5'5" and weighed maybe 130 lbs. She was a lovely girl with a petite figure and straight black hair falling down her back. She was also one of the most deadly women Tyson could find to guard his jewel when she wasn't with him. Claudia had insisted on being part of the hiring process when it came to her protection detail. She understood the necessity of having one, but she absolutely wasn't going to have Daniel dogging her every step.

While Daniel had warmed up to Claudia a tiny bit, in his own way, he still held himself stiffly separate. Claudia flat out refused to have decisions made for her when it came to her own safety. Tyson had been surprisingly understanding. He wanted his future wife to feel secure in her new life. When Daniel had gone toe to toe with Laney and pronounced her a decent fit for the security team, Claudia had hired her on the spot.

Claudia was still trying, after almost four months, to

break through the other woman's reserved exterior. Laney was polite, but distant. She watched Claudia's back like a mother hawk and seemed to care about her charge's happiness, but she never imparted anything personal about herself. A mystery Claudia was determined to get out of the other woman eventually.

Claudia reached for the box and opened it, but before she could look at the contents, she heard the bartender call for her. She exited the office with Laney on her heels. It didn't take long to see what Emile wanted her for. Boris, Sitnokov's personal bodyguard/possible butler, was striding through the club like he owned the place. When he spotted his quarry, he walked right up to her.

Laney reacted quickly by jumping in front of Claudia and snapping, "Stop where you are."

The giant Russian merely looked down at the much smaller girl and pushed her out of the way with an amused swat. He reached for Claudia and pulled her in for a quick, hard embrace. "Claudia," he said. *Clow-dee-yah.* "It is good to see you in health."

Claudia had no idea she was on hugging terms with Sitnikov's Russian beast. She wasn't sure if she should be terrified or flattered. Laney looked like she was about to attack the man with one of her swift and extremely painful takedowns (Claudia knew exactly how much it hurt, as Laney insisted she learn self-defence). Claudia stepped between the two and said calmly, "Can I help you Boris?"

He grunted, his eyes still lingering on the fuming woman behind Claudia's shoulder. "New place looks better," he said with a glance around.

Claudia raised a blond eyebrow. "I suppose you've come for a drink? We're not open until later tonight, but Emile can fix something for you."

He shook his head. "Boss wants to extend congratulations

to you and Mr. King on upcoming nuptials. He accepts your wedding invitation and looks forward to happy event."

Claudia, well aware that no such invitation had been extended, chose her words carefully. "Please tell Mr. Sitnikov... Vladimir... that we are honoured by his acceptance and look forward to the pleasure of his company. I will have Tyson's secretary forward the details."

Boris didn't say another word and effectively dismissed Claudia from his mind by stepping around her and getting into Laney's space. Laney gasped and took a quick step back, which wasn't something Claudia had ever seen her do before. Laney was wearing her hair in two french braids. The ends of the braids brushed against her shoulders. Boris reached out and rubbed the soft, black hair between his fingertips.

"You look like schoolgirl escaped from convent. How old are you?" he asked, staring intently down at the woman.

Laney smacked his hand from her hair. Her dark brown eyes glittered up at him angrily. "That's none of your damn business. Now step off big man," she snapped.

Claudia's breath caught in her throat as Boris stiffened. His body language told a story of instant death. There was just no way Laney could stand a chance against Boris in a fair fight. She was so much smaller than him. She would likely be faster, but that would only help if she were in a position to run away. Something Claudia suspected wasn't in Laney's repertoire.

Finally Boris said, "Maybe I will make it my business."

With a nod in Claudia's direction he turned and left. Claudia was expecting Laney to ask about Boris, but she just retreated without another word, maintaining her usual silence. Claudia wondered what that was all about. She would give Tyson Sitnikov's message later. He could sort out whatever it was Sitnikov wanted with them.

Claudia turned back to her office and went to open the

box Laney had brought in. A smile spread across her lips when she saw it was the new glassware she had ordered with the club's brand on them. The lettering 'underground' was distinct, like a masculine scrawl, but the glasses themselves were tall and flute-like. Claudia loved them. She had chosen them along with everything else associated with her new club, The Underground. This place was Tyson's engagement gift to her. His only stipulation being that she couldn't run the place until it was a legitimate business.

Claudia had happily accepted and immediately enrolled herself in business classes at the local college. Tyson had been amused by her enthusiasm until he saw the changes taking place in the seedy gambling club himself. Then he had started paying closer attention, proud of Claudia's natural business acumen. He had even approached her about potentially sitting on the board for King Trust. She said she would think about it once she finished college.

The paperwork for The Underground had gone through two weeks ago and the soft open was in a few hours. She had prepared for the evening before coming to the club, anticipating that she wouldn't have time later. She had been correct. She had spent the past few hours drilling new staff on their duties, drilling old staff on what to keep an eye out for at the tables and putting out various fires.

Claudia glanced in the mirror behind her desk and looked over her outfit with a critical eye. As the manager of the town's newest, trendiest gaming establishment, she had decided to go with an eye-popping gold thigh length cocktail dress. The high neck in front and sleeves made it respectable, the plunging back told a different story. Claudia had left her hair long, but swept the blond waves to the side in a clip to leave her back bare. She was currently wearing comfortable flats, but had brought strappy golden heels studded in crystals for later.

She had her back to the door and was leaning over her desk, reaching for her day planner to go over a few more details when a delicious, deep voice rumbled behind her, "Let's ditch the party, baby, and take that outfit back to my place where it belongs."

Grinning, Claudia leaned a little further across her desk, thrusting her ass out and wiggling her hips a little. She peeked at him over her shoulder and batted her heavily mascaraed eyelashes at him. "But I bought this dress specifically for the party, Mr. King. What will my dedicated employees think if the boss doesn't show up for opening night?"

Claudia's smile widened when she heard the door slam shut and the lock engage. She had argued with him about his insistence that the windows to her office be blacked out from the rest of the club, until he had shown exactly why he wanted it that way. Claudia had been much, much more pliable after her third or fourth orgasm.

She sighed happily when he came up behind her and slid one muscular forearm across her belly and the other around her throat, dragging her off the desk and pulling her up against his chest. Claudia tipped her head to the side and offered him her lips. He took them with a growl and, ignoring her perfect makeup, proceeded to ravish her mouth with all the pent up hunger he felt for her when he was forced to stay away while they both worked.

"Tyson!" she gasped when he took her by the back of the neck and forced her facedown over her desk once more. "I have to work!"

"Work can wait," he grunted, reaching under the short skirt of her dress and yanking her thong down to her ankles. He pushed the skirt up until her ass was bared to him.

"Fuck, babe, I never stop wanting this," he said caressing

long fingers down the crease of her ass and sinking them into her already wet pussy.

"Oh, fuck it!" Claudia moaned arching her back and widening her legs to give him better access to her.

Tyson pumped his fingers in and out of her with the hard penetrating strokes she loved so much. His fingertips massaged her g-spot until she was thrusting back against him and crying out in supplication. Later, she would be glad he had also insisted on soundproofing her office. Apparently he found the no nonsense business side of Claudia's personality extremely sexy.

"Oh god, Tyson, please just fuck me now," Claudia cried out, clutching the edge of her desk and shoving her hips back to meet his strokes.

"Yes, ma'am," he replied. He lowered the zip on his pants and pulled himself free of his boxers. His cock stood long and hard, ready to take a piece of his woman.

Tyson gave it to her the way she loved it, impaling himself full length into her silken heat. He gripped her hips in long fingers and yanked her back, ruthlessly forcing her to take every last inch. She moaned and bucked underneath him as she tried to absorb the pain and pleasure. He gave her a moment and then starting fucking her from behind.

"Look, Claudia," he grunted, reaching a hand out and palming the back of her head. He tugged until she was looking into the mirror behind her desk. She moaned breathlessly at the erotic sight and arched her back, thrusting her breasts out.

Tyson reached out with the intention of baring her breasts. Realizing he meant to tear her brand new and extremely expensive dress Claudia grabbed the hand that reached for her and bit down, chomping her small white teeth into the fleshy part of his hand. Tyson stiffened against her back and stopped thrusting into her.

He grabbed her hair and yanked her head back. He dropped his face into her neck and bit down, "You like it rough, do you, woman?"

She nodded, gasping for breath, "God yes! Please, fuck me hard Tyson!"

Tyson obliged her, pressing one hand hard against her back and forcing her to lay across the desk while he used the other hand to grip her hip. He fucked her with everything he had, loving the way her soft pink body took everything he gave her. Tyson bent his knees and slammed himself into her welcoming pussy until he could no longer hold out. With a final savage thrust, he buried himself deep into her passage and reached around to rub her clit in slow, hard circles until she was bucking wildly under him and screaming her orgasm.

While she drifted back to reality, Tyson reached down and pulled her panties back up, tugged her skirt down and picked her up in his arms. She smiled dreamily up at him as he sat down on the nearby leather couch he had also suggested. Arranging her across his thighs he held her close, running his big hands down her arm and across her back. Finally, he picked up her hand and laced his fingers through hers. He lifted her left hand up and kissed the flesh next to the ring he had placed on her finger.

"This ring is the only reason I'm letting you wear this damn dress in public, you know that, right?"

Claudia laughed. "If anyone attacks me, it'll be to steal this rock you put on my finger, not to get at what's under this dress. You're the only one that has that particular obsession."

"I seriously doubt that," he replied, relaxing into the sofa cushions and pulling her up against his chest. They listened to the banging on the office door in contented silence for a moment before he spoke, "I'm surprised she still does that after the first few times we locked ourselves in here."

"That's why we pay her the big bucks," Claudia said with a

smile, tracing her fingers over the new tattoo, the word Queen, inked onto his taut forearm. "It's her job to worry over my whereabouts. It's only a matter of time before she finally manages to steal my key, get a copy made and interrupt us *in flagrante*."

"It's her own damn fault then if she sees my massive dick and runs screaming. Your bodyguard looks like some kind of schoolgirl nun cross. She could probably use an eyeful or a good fuck to shock her out of her prudish ninja nun thing."

Claudia thumped him on the chest, "That's what Boris called her."

He arched a brow at her and she said, "Long story. I'll tell you later. Now remind me of how much you love me and how you've written endless amounts of shoes for your new bride into our marriage contract?"

"Insatiable woman," he said with a grin and kissed her waiting lips.

THE END

NIKITA'S NEWSLETTER!

Sign up today for Nikita's newsletter and receive a FREE copy of Nikita's bestselling dark romance novella, Stalked! CLICK HERE to sign up today!

BONUS: MAFIA'S SAVAGE OBSESSION

"I asked you a question, Sitnikov," she spat his name like it was a curse. "What do you want?"

His thin lips curled up in a cruel smile – though, to be fair, she didn't think the hard slash of his mouth was made for anything other than cruel expressions. "Ah, Jane, now *that* is a question with many answers. Few that I think you would enjoy quite yet." He leaned back, his chair creaking against the worn tile of her kitchen floor.

Jane rolled her eyes. "I'm definitely not in the mood for word games, Sitnikov. Why *the fuck* are you here, in my home? One would think that you'd prefer to keep your distance from the cop that's about to take you down."

His eyes narrowed slightly, but otherwise his expression didn't change. "You have a smart mouth, Jane, you should be careful what you say with it, lest a concerned citizen step in to shut those lovely lips," he remarked quietly. "Call me Vladimir."

"Not in this lifetime, *Sit-ni-kov*," she sneered, pronouncing each syllable of his last name deliberately. "Also, I'm pretty sure that was a threat you were uttering. You might want to step lightly while in the presence of a police officer and her gun. I'm pretty sure it wouldn't be too difficult to claim self-defence if a suspected mob boss were shot in my apartment."

A muscle in his strong jaw jumped. The sudden tightening of his body was barely perceptible, except to the eyes of an experienced cop. She'd spent enough time in the interrogation room to know when a man was stopping himself from lunging across the table toward her. She almost smirked at the thought of getting a reaction out of a man like Sitnikov. She really did have a remarkable tendency to piss people off. It was how she had made detective at such a young age. Her dogged determination combined with her take-no-prisoners attitude had impressed the higher ups. Plus, she pissed off her beat sergeant to the point where he was happy to see her promoted and out of his department.

"I have an offer for you," Sitnokov said, his dark eyes drinking her in.

She arched her eyebrow. "This should be good."

"Be my mistress."

Jane sat frozen in her chair caught between laughter at the absurdity of his proposition, and terror. "That's the stupidest thing I've ever heard. You would let a cop get that close to you? Just to scratch an itch? You like to live dangerously, don't you, Sitnikov? Sure, yeah, let's do it. Can we go back to your place now? Can I have the code to your safe before we get down?"

His lips curled in a quasi smile at her sarcasm. "No, I would not allow a police detective access to my private life," he said calmly.

Jane frowned. "I don't understand. Supposedly you want to have a fling with me, a *detective*, but you don't plan on letting law enforcement near you. I'm not sure how long it's been for you, but usually that kind of intimacy requires a physical presence. Not that I'm even remotely entertaining the idea of any kind of relationship with you. Not happening, *Russian*." She spat the last word.

He didn't seem to enjoy the way she spoke to him. His body was rigid in the seat and he seemed to be struggling with himself. She was happy to have a weapon close at hand. She suspected that no one spoke to the Boss the way she just had. Or if they did, they quickly found themselves without a tongue and having silent conversations with fishes. She had to bite her own tongue just from pointing out her original assertion that she tended to annoy people.

"Listen to my offer, then give your opinion, *woman*." He deliberately sneered the last word. His posture was relaxed, but his eyes were sharp, taking in every expression that crossed her features. "You will quit your job and come to live with me. For a time, we will share a home and a bed. I will pay you a monthly fee that will make your current salary look like a child's allowance. I will also give you a generous settlement and a house once we have finished our association."

Jane's breath caught in her chest and pain blossomed. She felt sudden and intense hatred for the man sitting across from her. It made her feel out of control, something she hadn't felt for years. Not one to hide her feelings, Jane reached out and picked up the gun. She pointed it at him, flipped the safety off and said, "We're done with this conversation. You can go now."

His dark eyes snapped in fury before he hid it under his usual icy visage. "You do not like my terms, though they are more than generous? Name what it is you want then, I may be willing to negotiate."

Jane clenched her teeth and spoke in a furious voice. "I *want* you to admit to the murder of Dennis Yankovich. On record. Then I *want* you to go rot in a federal prison somewhere for the rest of your life. In the mean time, you can take your offer and go fuck yourself."

He thought for a moment, his body straining in his seat, and then shook his head slightly. "I don't think I will accommodate that request, no matter how attractive I find you. Put the gun down, Jane. I don't want you to get hurt."

"Fuck you, Sitnikov. Get out of my apartment. Now!" she snapped. "The answer is no. You don't get to touch me, *ever*."

Sitnikov stood, his long limbs unfolding with the fluidity of a lion rising from rest. Jane stood also, not wanting to feel small or trapped around this predatory man. He stalked around the table toward her. His lean, muscular body tensed with lethal intent. Jane brought the gun up, her grip steady and professional. She snapped, "Stop, don't you come near me!"

Rather than waste time responding, Sitnikov stepped swiftly to the side, forcing her to bring her gun arm around. Before the gun settled on him again, he reached out and gripped her wrist in a ruthless hold that made her cry out, and yanked the gun from her grip with his other hand. He moved so quickly Jane didn't have a chance. He flipped the safety back on and tossed the gun in the direction of her couch.

"No!" she gasped as he took hold of her arms and hauled her bodily up against his hard chest.

Jane reacted quickly, twisting in his arms, attempting to break his hold. He lifted her easily off the ground, giving her less space to fight in. Jane slammed her forehead into his face, aiming for his nose. He moved his head to the side, but she still managed to score a solid hit.

Sitnikov grunted, his cheek and mouth taking the brunt of her hit. His lip split against his tooth and blood spurted down his chin. He twisted her in his arms so her back was pressed against his chest.

"Enough!" he growled.

"You promised you wouldn't hurt me!" Jane snarled, struggling in his unbreakable hold.

"I have no intention of hurting you, Jane." His voice was deep and steady against her ear, despite the hit she'd meted out. "But you mistake my intention in coming here. The offer is not contingent on your acceptance. The offer is a bonus for what is inevitable. You *will* become my mistress."

He turned her to face him again, his fingers tightening around her arms. He lifted her up until only the tips of her bare toes touched the floor and she was forced to brace her hands against his hard body for stability. She felt the flexed pectoral muscles under his expensive shirt. His heart beat steadily against her fingertips. He dropped his face towards hers, his lips inches from her mouth. He ignored the blood dripping steadily down his chin and onto his shirt collar.

Their breaths mingled as tension snapped in the air around them. He smelled like mint with a hint of cigar and vodka. She braced herself against his chest, her fingers digging into the muscles, as she tried ineffectively to push him away. She tried kicking him, but he moved faster, kicking her legs apart and shoving his legs between hers.

Every self defence maneuver she tried was countered and subdued. She was out of options and trapped in his hold. He seemed to enjoy her fight. There was nothing she could do to stop him. "I don't want your offer, my answer is no. Now go away!" she hissed. "I knew you were pathetic, Sitnikov, but I had no idea how much. Is this the only way you can pick up women?"

He laughed shortly and tilted his head until his nose touched the damp, sweet-smelling hair just above her ear, smearing blood on her freshly washed skin. He inhaled and said in a deep voice, "I'm giving you the choice to quit your job at the police service, Jane McKinley. Walk away now and

I will reward you. I have money. I can buy you beautiful things. At my side you will know only respect and fine things."

"No!" she snapped. "You're out of your mind, you fucking psychopath!"

He yanked her up onto her toes and bent his head until their faces nearly touched. He appeared to reach for patience, his lips thinning. "I am giving you this one chance to accept my offer. It is... how do you say... a one-time deal, little cop. If you do not accept now, then you will suffer the consequences of coming to my bed in a much less honourable way."

"Fuck you!" she snarled trying to rear back.

"In good time."

"Not in this fucking lifetime you motherfucking son of a bitch. Let me the fuck go!" she snarled at him, her rage and fear making her more reckless than she might have otherwise been in the presence of a criminal boss who had her alone and at his mercy.

Jane tried to lunge backwards in hopes of knocking him off balance enough so she could go for the gun. She didn't even care if it looked like self defence any more, she was going to empty that gun into his male chauvinistic ass, reload and then shoot her initials into him. He gripped her by the back of the robe and yanked. The robe was wrenched down her arms trapping them at her side and exposing the pale skin and small rounded breasts of her upper body.

He took a handful of her black hair and pulled her head back in a brutal grip. He dropped his head so she could see his dark eyes. They finally showed some emotion, a terrible kind of anger mixed with intense lust. The blood on his mouth and chin gave his already terrifying visage an extra sinister twist.

"You will treat me with respect, woman, or you will find out why I am the most feared man in this city." He didn't need to raise his voice to make his message clear. "I am in control now and I will tell you something that I have told no one before."

"What?" she snapped, her voice quavering slightly.

"You test my control."

His words were simple, but chilling. They were enough to ensure her silence for the moment.

"I have killed men. I have beaten and broken men. I have destroyed them and done so with extreme control. I never do anything without control." His breathing altered, becoming more rapid. As he continued, his voice took on a savage edge. "But you, my fuckable little police woman, test my control. I want things I should not want with you. I want to lose my control with you. I want to keep you, own you, *hurt you*."

Jane's breath caught in her throat. "You don't scare me," she lied. She shivered, a chill coursing across her bared breasts, causing goosebumps to break out and her nipples to harden.

He laughed. Unpleasantly. Chillingly. "You should be afraid, woman. Because I have never denied myself something I have wanted."

She stilled completely and ever so slightly pulled her body away from any contact with his.

"Da, I see you comprehend."

She nodded, daring a look up at him. "What are you going to do?"

He stared down at her for a moment, his gaze sweeping her throat, breasts and belly with scorching heat, and then allowed the tiniest of frowns to mar his otherwise expressionless cold face. "I am going to deny myself, just this once – for both of our sakes. I will walk away from you, Jane McKinley. I will give you the chance to have your shining career without my interference."

"I repeat, what do you want from me?"

"You need to disappear from my sight, Jane. You need to make yourself scarce." He spoke next to her ear causing a shiver to trace down her spine. As if he couldn't help himself, he followed that shiver with one long finger. "You will not seek me out again and you will drop the Dennis Yankovich line of questioning that involves me."

Jane had known why he was there from the start. He was threatening her in an elemental way to drop the case against him. She had experienced this before. As a small, attractive female policewoman she had endured her share of rape threats. None quite like this, but she was experienced enough to understand where he was going with this.

The predictability infuriated her. She wanted to rage at him. Why couldn't a man just want her for herself, not for what she represented? Not to fuck away a policewoman's sense of power.

"What if I don't?" she spit out glaring up into his face.

His actions were swift and ruthless.

Jane barely managed a gasp when he pulled her hair back, forcing her to arch her neck and back, thrusting out her gorgeous, rounded breasts. He devoured her without further touch. She suddenly felt as small as he wanted her to feel and tried to shrink away from him. He wouldn't allow it and dragged her closer, his eyes tracing her pale breasts down across her flat stomach to her strong thighs still hidden beneath the folds of her robe. She struggled, but he shook her viciously, causing her head to swim.

"If you do not obey me, there will be consequences, officer McKinley. Consequences you will not enjoy, I promise," he snapped. "You have declined my generous offer and I have kindly decided to back off, for now. If you continue down your current path, I will give myself free reign to indulge what I am now holding back for your sake. I am not a lover. I am a killer and a loner, a man better left alone. I enjoy hurting other people, Detective. If you pursue me, then I will end the chase my way. I will take you, put you in a cage and I will keep you for my exclusive and particular use. In short, I will break you."

His words were so rapid and so accented she had trouble following them. But she understood the gist. "Are you threatening me?"

"*Yes*, Jane, I am most definitely threatening you," he agreed. "But the question is, will you take heed, or will you continue on this reckless course you seem so intent on?"

She remained silent. She believed him. But she wouldn't stop. She was close to pinning Yankovich's murder on him. And now she could add threatening a police officer to his charges.

As if reading her mind, he gave her the cold smile that seemed to be his signature. "You are very easy to read, my pet," he said, stroking the hair back from her temple. She jerked her head away, but he ignored the small defiance. "If you must have it your way then I will choose to look forward to the hunt with anticipation."

Releasing his grip, he reached down to cover her exposed curves. His fingers shook very slightly, betraying how close to the edge of his control he had reached. She wondered if perhaps, maybe a little, she did test his legendary icy calm. The image of herself forced into slavery to this man sent a shudder rippling through her small frame. Sitnikov smoothed a hand down the front of her robe ensuring it was in place and her modesty was intact.

"Goodbye, my pet." His deep, accented voice caressed her. "And forget I exist. It is perhaps better... for both of us."

She said nothing. The scariest man she had ever crossed paths with turned and left. She briefly considered shooting him in the back, but was too shaky to go after the gun. Legs wobbling, she sunk to the floor of her small apartment, wrapped her arms around her knees and allowed weakness to wash over her. She touched the spot behind her ear that his lips and nose had caressed, and her fingers came away wet with his blood.

Keep reading Mafia's Savage Obsession!

BONUS: MERCENARY'S DARK OBSESSION

He didn't believe in telepathy or the unexplained. He thought if there wasn't an explanation for something, then that explanation just hadn't been discovered yet. The fact that he knew Addison Sterling was standing down the hall on the other side of a solid steel door from where he stood was simply heightened senses and intuition. He was in tune with this woman's every movement, every breath, every heartbeat. He imagined, if he closed his eyes he would know at any given moment where she stood in her apartment. Right now she was preparing to leave, like she did every morning at the same time. If she belonged to him, he would break her of that dangerous habit.

Lucky for her, she would never belong to him.

She stepped out of her door and turned gracefully on her ballet flats, her long white and blue pattered dress swishing around her legs. Her long, slim fingers unerringly found the lock on the door, where she inserted the key as she'd done a thousand times and turned it. Dropping the key into a small knit purse, which was strapped across her body, separating the lovely mounds of her breasts over the elasticized top of her summer dress. She bent her knees and reached to pick up the leather case containing her cello.

As he did every morning when he came down to her floor, he ruthlessly stopped himself from reaching out to snatch the case from her, the muscles under his shirt bunching in anger. The case was too big for her. She was too fragile. She loved it too much, far more than she loved anything else. He wanted to take it from her and destroy it. Which confused him. He didn't usually have impulse control issues.

She strode confidently toward the elevator, stopping only steps from where he stood, and reached for the button, her fingers so close to his stomach she nearly touched him. He planned it that way, imagined for a second what it would feel like if she did touch him. The elevator dinged, letting her know it had arrived. She waited for approximately three heartbeats and then stepped forward as the doors swished back. He stepped out in unison. As the doors closed, she turned to face them. He used the sound of the elevators closing to move swiftly around her.

Confident she was alone, she relaxed her stance, allowing her shoulders to soften. He stood so close to her back that if she'd leaned just a little she would've touched him. It was worth the risk for him to be able to reach out and touch the ends of her soft, wavy chestnut hair. To lean in close and smell the delicate tropical, flowery lotion she used on her skin after her morning shower. He inhaled deeply, savouring her scent, imagining her in the marble bathroom of her condo, naked, rubbing the hemp lotion over her curves in circular motions, as was her routine.

In his desperation to be near Addison, he must've gotten closer than he'd dared before, because she suddenly went rigid beneath the shadow of his body. Her face snapped to the side, her lips nearly brushing his where he'd bent into her neck. Her blank, dark eyes were wide with apprehension.

He stopped breathing. Not for fear of being caught. He was more than capable of taking down a dozen mercenaries, let alone one small blind woman. No, he needed to protect her. For some reason he cared for Addison Sterling, and if he got involved with her, he would hurt her, probably irreparably. The black part of his soul already called for him to reach out and grab her, to make her beg, to subjugate her, to hunt, hurt and humiliate her. Already, he couldn't leave her alone. He'd never experienced such driving need to possess a woman. At best he usually considered them unnecessary distractions that he usually avoided.

Somehow Addison was different.

"Is someone there?" she whispered, the sweet warmth of her breath rushing over him.

His cock answered her, though he stayed silent. His pupils dilated and he vibrated with the effort not to grab her, pin her to the wall of the elevator, tear her ugly dress away, force her onto her knees and enjoy the fear in her eyes while he took that beautiful mouth of hers.

The door dinged and Addison jumped, her head snapping forward once more. She visibly shook herself, pushing her shoulders back and forcing her confidence back on like a cloak of independence she wore whenever she left her apartment. "Stupid Addie," she said beneath her breath, before stepping off the elevator. He watched her like the predator he was as she shook open her white walking cane, smiled and cheerfully greeted the concierge. The elevator doors closed, cutting off his view of her. He wanted to go after her. To follow her and speak to her like a normal man would.

He couldn't. He was a savage through and through. He'd seen and done things normal men couldn't even imagine.

That was why he was Tyson King's head of security. That was why he couldn't have Addison Sterling.

Unfortunately for her, he couldn't seem to let her go. Her lush curves, delicate beauty and helpless attempts at independence called to the predator in him like nothing else. He knew, eventually, he would answer that call.

Keep reading Mercenary's Dark Obsession

ALSO BY NIKITA SLATER

If you enjoyed this book, check out some other works by USA Today Bestselling Author, Nikita Slater. More titles are always in progress, so check back often to see what's new!

IMMORTAL WOLF SHIFTERS

Book 1 - Damaged Mate

Book 2 - The Witch and the Wolf - Coming soon!

Book 3 - Wolf's Eternal Mate - Coming soon!

Book 4 - Protected by Her Mate - Coming soon!

Book 5 - The King's Mate - Coming soon!

SINNER'S EMPIRE

Book 1 - Sin of Silence

Book 2 - A Silent Reckoning

Book 3 - Goodnight, Sinners

Sinner's Empire Complete Trilogy

THE QUEENS SERIES

Book One – Scarred Queen

Book Two - Queen's Move

Book Three - Born a Queen

Book Four - The Red Queen

Book 5 - The Queen's Bodyguard (coming soon!)

Alejandro's Prey (a novella)

The Queens 4 Book Box Set

AGENTS OF CASA DE FLORES SERIES

Book One – Lotus

Book Two - Rose (Coming soon!)

KINGS OF THE UNDERWORLD

Billionaire's Captive Mistress

Mafia's Savage Obsession

Mafia's Savage Boss

Mercenary's Dark Obsession

Bratva's Captive Assassin

Bounty Hunter's Innocent Prize

Italian's Captive Beauty

Bodyguard's Forbidden Obsession

THE DRIVEN HEARTS SERIES

Book One - Driven by Desire

Book Two - Thieving Hearts

Book Three - Capturing Victory

Novella - The Princess and Her Mercenary

Driven Hearts 4 Book Box Set

THE SANCTUARY SERIES

Book One - Sanctuary's Warlord

Book Two - Sanctuary on Fire

Book Three - The Last Sanctuary

Book Four - The Road to Wolfe

Book Five - Skye's Sanctuary

The Sanctuary Series 3 Book Box Set

LOVING THE BAD BOY SERIES

Loving Vincent

Loving Jared

Loving Rico (Coming Soon!)

STANDALONE BOOKS

The Assassin's Wife

Because You're Mine

Luna & Andres

Kiss of the Cartel

Stalked

Toxic Love Story - Coming soon!

Visit ***nikitaslater.com*** for more information

and the latest updates!

STAY CONNECTED WITH NIKITA!

Don't miss one dark and sexy moment. Keep in touch with Nikita for her latest news and updates about all of your favourite characters!

- Get more info and updates on Nikita's **Website**
- Like and follow me on **Facebook**
- Follow me on **TikTok**
- Check out my **Instagram**
- Connect with me on **Goodreads**

Sign up for the newsletter today at receive exclusive updates and access to ***bonus content and chapters*** not available anywhere else!

https://www.authornikitaslater.com/

ABOUT NIKITA SLATER

Nikita Slater is the USA Today Bestselling Author of action-packed suspenseful romance. She writes dark romance, mafia romance, and post-apocalyptic dystopian romance. She lives on the beautiful Canadian prairies with her son and her crazy awesome dog. She has an unholy affinity for books, wine, pets and anything chocolate. Despite some of the darker themes in her books (which are pure fun and fantasy), Nikita is a staunch feminist and advocate of equal rights for all races, genders and non-gender specific persons. When she isn't writing, dreaming about writing or talking about writing, she helps others discover a love of reading and writing through literacy and social work.

For more information about Nikita and her work, please see her website at www.authornikitaslater.com.